HALLBOYS

SIX STORIES

SHORT STORIES
FROM BOYS HALL in NO PALMS

BY
MICHAEL DASWICK

ISBN #9781513650890

Scottsdale Arizona

Copyright © August, 2019

By Michael Daswick

PLAYA CHICA PRESS

No Palms, California

No Palms is a fictional town.

Boys Hall is a fictional orphanage.

Chip Rock is a fictional young man.

These stories and their characters are, therefore, works of fiction.

Table of Contents

BIILLY the BRAIN'S SOCIAL EXPERIMENT

Betty Battle gave us the stink eye as she came out of the candy shop on the Pacific Ocean Parkway in No Palms. Thirty minutes later we'd find her purse underneath the bus stop bench.

Ordinarily, Hallboys like us would've obeyed the honor code and returned the lost item in a heartbeat. Even if it belonged to Betty Battle of the No Palms Women's Club. Everybody at the Hall, and in No Palms, knew that nobody in the whole wide world, living or dead, hated Hallboys more than Betty Battle. This case, however, created a giant conundrum and led to Billy the Brain's seventh grade social experiment. We didn't rush to return Betty's purse. Not after we found $1,100 in it. In cash. Here's what happened.

*****

Sunday afternoon. Cal and Billy and I were in the middle of our customary walk downtown. With no particular destination in mind, there was a good chance we'd wind up at the Little Store, the boardwalk, the pier, El Burger Bucket, and scanning the beach and Park for chicks.

Betty Battle, president of the No Palms Women's Club, must've been in a good mood that Sunday afternoon. We saw her go inside the candy shop at the center of town on the P.O.P. We sat on the curb nearby fixing a skateboard and watched through the window as she selected six chocolate covered marshmallows, eight double fudge caramel turtles, ten vanilla dipped strawberries, and a dozen butterscotch pretzels. As she left she stumbled right into us on the sidewalk.

"Hi Miss Battle," Cal said, politely. "Happen to have any extra candy for three famished Hallboys?"

Betty instinctively clutched her candy bag tight to her bosom. "My goodness *No!*" she grumped, flashing us the sour puss. She spun away and turned down the sidewalk. Billy the Brain waved goodbye as she hurried away.

We fixed the skateboard and took a quick look-see on the pier. Then we pooled our change and bought a mega-malt at El Burger Bucket. Horsing around a bit on the P.O.P., Cal chased a fat seagull but tripped and landed flat on his face, on the sidewalk. And there it was. Underneath the bus stop bench. A purse. A heavy leather ladies purse, with two handles, shiny side panels, gusseted ends, and a brass clasp at the top. Just lying there under the bus stop bench. A fat pink one.

"Guys, look!" Cal whispered. "A *handbag!*"

We stared at it.

"Oh, man!" cries Billy the Brain, dropping to his knees next to Cal.

"Grab it," I said.

Cal grabbed the purse by its handles and looked at me and Billy.

"Come on! Run! *To the cliffs!*"

We dashed. Down the street, across the boardwalk, past the pier, and up the winding path that led to the top of cliffs above No Palms cove. It was our favorite spot in town, far above the sea where the waves slammed the rocks below.

We ran til we got to the shady side of the old abandoned lighthouse and fell to our knees.

"Whose do you think it is?" I asked, panting.

"Dunno," Billy says. "Dump it out."

Cal spilled the contents onto the dirt next to the lighthouse rocks. "Man O man," Cal said. "Look at all the junk!"

We stared at the pile. There was a whole mess of stuff. Slowly, Billy reached for a red wallet, and undid the snap. The driver's license was right on top.

"Holee shit," Billy whispered. "Guess what! It's Betty's"

"Betty *Battle?*"

"Yep. Old prune-face herself. Dang. We just found Betty Battle's purse. Holee crap!" Billy passed the driver's license to me. It was Betty's all right, complete with a photo which included her signature scowl.

Betty Battle was of course arch enemy number one of every Hallboy. It had been that way for years, certainly as long as I could remember, ever since I was old enough to know how nasty a Women's Clubber could be. I'm almost sure that when I first learned the swear word that started with a B, it was in association with Betty Battle.

Betty hated Boys Hall. And she hated Hallboys. Why? Nobody knew. But she hated us. And in turn, we were at war with her. And her crappy Women's Club.

"Look at all this stuff. She's got so much crap!"

We went through everything. Picking through the big stuff first, Billy tugged at an old lady scarf and a long envelope slid out. We stared at it. Cal picked it up and showed us the big letters on the front. "**Bingo 101**".

Then Cal peeked inside the envelope. His mouth opened but no words came out. Then he said, "Dudes. Whoa! It's full of money! And it's a *fortune*." Cal held up a wad of bills an inch thick. Twenties, tens and fives. More money than we'd ever seen in our entire Hallboy lives. We counted it. $1,100.

"That makes sense," I said. "Saturday night is bingo night over there. This is their take."

Cal dropped the money in the dirt. "That's a serious fortune!"

"It's like a treasure."

"I ain't never seen so much money. Ever!"

There was a slip of paper nestled in with the bills. Cal unfolded the slip. There, written in an old lady's hand:

4 quart bottles Gin

3 bots vodka

3 bots bourbon whiskey

6 bots red wine

6 bots white wine (dry)

2 bots Sherry

1 bot peach schnapps

1 crème de menthe

1 vermouth

2 Brandy

2 Scotch

1 Rum (light)

1 Rum (dark)

Tequila

6 tonic

6 soda

"Guys! It's a list of booze! All different kinds! Booze for the old bats at the Club!"

"Their bingo money goes to pay for their booze."

"Betty was off to fill the liquor cabinet."

"Guys," said Billy the Brain. "Listen to me. First of all, this is a woman's purse. That's like, *sooo important* to them. It's not as if someone lost a toothpick here. A purse is like an anatomical part of their arms. Grown women take their purses to the bathroom with them. I know that. If Betty lost her purse, she'll be looking for it in a *nanosecond*. Especially with all this dough inside. And she'll tear this town apart until she finds it."

"What the heck are we gonna do?"

"I'm thinking."

"Brain," Cal aid with hesitation, "are we gonna keep it?"

"Lemme think, okay?"

Normally, of course, returning any lost and found item to its rightful owner was a Hallboy no-brainer. This was fundamental doctrine. Honesty. Instilled within each and every Hallboy from day one, before we learned how to hold a fork, before we learned how to pee pee by ourselves. Part of the Honor Code. Give it back, it's the right thing to do. It's the only thing to do. You might get a reward, you might not, but that was entirely beside the point

Billy grabbed the cash and shoved it back in its envelope. "Dudes," he said. "We tell *nobody*. Got it? We don't tell *anybody* about this."

"Right. Of course not."

"Aren't we gonna give it back?" Cal asked.

Billy took the money back out and counted it again.

"We can give back the purse, but keep the money," Cal suggested timidly.

Billy looked at Cal. It was almost a *glare*.

"Or, if we return the whole thing, maybe there's a reward," Cal said next.

"Guys, I'm thinking, okay?" Billy sighed. I could tell he was disappointed that his brain wasn't working too fast. Then he said, "Let's see what else is in here."

We sorted through the rest of it. In her purse, Betty had a receipt for two dozen doughnuts from Dolly's Donut Den. She had a halfway done role of breath mints; a pair of plastic granny glasses, in a pink vinyl case; a mirrored makeup compact (Billy spilled the powder on his jeans); bobby pins; two teenie teenie bottles of gin, both empty; three pens; an almost-gone pack of Kleenex; several *used* Kleenex, balled up and damp. That was gross. Nail file. One dry old French fry; nail polish (rosy –red); Polygrip; comb; a dusty old brush stuck full of gray hairs; lipsticks; Jolly ranchers; peppermints; tootsie rolls; half of a 3 Musketeers bar, Q-tips; tweezers; a teenie breath spray, three plastic packets of mayonnaise; a small photo case with wrinkled snapshots of some old dude, two girls, and three shots of the fattest cat we'd ever seen.

We rifled through Betty Battle's billfold. Besides the driver's license there were credit cards, a bunch of papers, library card, 34 dollars in cash, parking ticket, Social Security card, a folded paper with many phone numbers on it, and several sticks of Juicy Fruit hidden in the last pocket. There were quarters, dimes, and nickels in the change compartment.

The last item was a large tube of hemorrhoid cream.

"I've never seen more junk in my life," says Cal.

"Remember, you guys," Billy looked at us. "We ain't telling nobody. We'd get killed."

"Are we gonna keep anything?"

"I'm thinking…" Billy said.

"As soon as Betty finds out she doesn't have her purse, she'll poop her pants."

"You're right," Billy said, standing up and handing the **Bingo 101** envelope to Cal. "Come on. We gotta hurry. Throw all this crap back inside the purse."

"The money too?"

"Yeah. Until I figure out what to do."

We loaded everything back inside.

"Where we going now?"

"Burger Bucket. C'mon."

Billy ran down the hill with Cal and I right behind. Cal carried the pink purse out in front of him like it was covered in tuberculosis germs. We reached El Burger Bucket, directly across the street from the candy shop and the bus stop bench.

"Keep a lookout," says Billy. "Duck down. And don't let anybody see that purse."

Sure enough, in minutes, Betty Battle appeared, lumbering quickly down the sidewalk with two other old biddies. They were in great haste.

"Here they come!"

I crouched beneath the window sill. Cal was ducked behind a chair. Billy pressed up against the wall, peering around the edge of the door.

Urgency and fret covered Betty's face. She cased the bus stop bench. She circled it, she looked up and down the gutter. She knelt down, shaking her head. She ran inside the candy shop, and ran back out. She checked the shop-fronts of three or four stores either side of the bench. She stooped down to look under the parked cars. She swore. She kicked the bench. Finally, she threw her hands in the air and clasped the sides of her head, no doubt to check and see if she had lost her mind. Then she and her buddies stormed away, off to the Women's Club. Billy the Brain rolled across the floor, laughing.

Sitting on the floor of El Burger Bucket, we felt like we'd just pulled a fast one on grumpy old Betty Battle, arch enemy of a generation of Hall-boys. Cal was still giggling, Billy alit with self-satisfaction. Of course, the fun was only beginning.

"She's hated us Hallboys our entire lives," Cal started. "What did we ever do to her?"

"Remember when we found that dead seal on the beach and we were dragging it out of the way cause it stunk so bad? She accused us of trying to take it to the Women's Club, to let it rot on their lawn. Golly, we never even thought of that."

"And the time she ran out of their clubhouse and grabbed Cal's skateboard? She said it was clattering on the sidewalk. Disturbing their meeting."

"The old bag."

"Three years ago. When we went to play <u>Clear the Pier</u>? We finally had all the seagulls shewed away and she ran out and confiscated our slingshots."

"Yeah! Then she burned them!"

"And gave the ashes to the Head of the Hall."

"He gave them back to us."

"We made mud pies with the ashes. And threw them at their house."

"Splato! That was cool."

"Fourth-grade. We slung up that tire swing underneath the pier. *That* was cool."

"Until big butt Betty when out with garden shears, and cut our rope."

"The tire sunk like a rock."

"And she laughed at us. Cackled like a witch."

"A witch with the letter B."

"And fifth grade. She was tending her flowers in the Park, when poor Ping-Pong walked by. All he did was pick his nose."

"She said he was giving her the finger. She hauled poor Ping-Pong straight off to the police station."

"The Head of the Hall had to come down. Lucky for Ping Pong he never believed a word of bad breath Betty's story. But she's still such a witch."

"So, Billy, what the heck are we gonna do?"

"I've got the plan," Billy announced.

Billy rose and got a paper sack from the guys working at the Bucket. "First," he said, "Cal, put the purse in this bag. We'll look pretty stupid walking around with a pink purse."

"Are we keeping the money?" I asked the question: "Eleven hundred bucks?"

Billy smiled.

"Are we keeping *some* of it?"

Billy glared.

"Hey! Let's put a dead Seagull inside the purse and toss it in their window."

Billy shook his head.

"We fill it full of sand."

"No."

"Dead fish?"

Billy shook his head again.

"We donate the money to the Hall?"

"Nope."

"Let's split it up with all the other guys!"

"Nope."

"Do we split it up, just among *ourselves*?"

"No."

"Take it to the cops?"

"Nope."

"Then what?"

Billy smiled. Then he started to nod his head up and down. Billy the Brain smacked a fist into his palm. *"We're gonna give it back."*

A wash of disappointment spread across our faces. "Really?"

"Yeah. Really."

"Ain't we gonna keep any of it?"

"No. Not a cent." Billy could see our disappointment. "But first, we're gonna put Buttermilk Betty in a very awkward position. Bingo 101 my butt. We're gonna hold us a social experiment."

*****

I don't know if Billy the Brain was the smartest Hallboy we had, but he sure could scheme. He laid out the plan. Over the next three days and nights, Cal and Billy and I went door-to-door to each and every Hallboy, young and old. We knocked on each room. We took up a collection.

Billy told us, "We're gonna ask everyone for two dollars. Each Hallboy has to contribute two bucks."

Every Hallboy asked us, "What for?".

"Don't ask any stupid questions. It's a social experiment. Pony up."

Some kids gave nothing. Some gave us $10. Most gave the two bucks. In the end, we had $725.

Billy counted it carefully, smoothing the bills, pressing them flat. Then he laid them inside Betty's "**Bingo 101**" envelope with the other money and the list of liquor.

Before there was $1,100. Now there was $1,825.

"It's a social experiment," Billy told us. "See? We give her back *extra*. Then we wait and see."

"Wait and see for what?"

"To see what happens. To see what she does."

"What are you expecting?"

"I have no idea. That's why it's an experiment."

Nobody wanted to doubt Billy the Brain. However, Cal and I looked at him with enormous skepticism.

"Look," Billy explained. "At a minimum we'll shame her into acknowledging an act of kindness from the Hallboys. Can you imagine how humiliating that'd be? For Betty Battle to have to admit to our graciousness, to accept our generosity towards her booze fund? She'll have to humble herself in front of us! She'd rather jump off the end of the pier in a bikini on the 4th of July."

Billy was smart. He took a photograph of all the money. And a photo of the purse. "Just in case."

"In case of what?"

"I have no idea."

We placed the envelope, fatter than ever, back inside Betty's purse.

"Cal," Billy said, "you take the purse back to Betty at the old ladies' club."

"Why me?"

"Because you're the one who found it. But don't worry, we'll be there watching. Walk right up the front steps like you're some really important delivery boy, and knock on the front door. Real polite and all. At lunchtime on Friday when everybody's inside."

"Do we include a note?"

Billy's eyes twinkled. "Of course we'll leave a note."

"What do we say? Do we give her our names?"

"No. Anonymous. She'll have to seek us out, she'll have to make some *inquiries*. That's part of the social experiment."

"What do we say in the note?"

Billy wrote out the note on notebook paper.

FOUND THIS NICE PURSE NEAR THE CANDY SHOP. RE-TURNING IT TO ITS RIGHTFUL OWNER. EXACTLY AS IT WAS FOUND.
WITH FONDNESS,
YOUR FRIENDS AT BOYS HALL.

"And you know what else?" Billy went on. "It ain't gonna be no ordinary note. We're gonna write it *in icing*. On top of a big cake. That'll get their attention."

The next evening after supper we went to the great kitchen in the dining hall. Hallboys were never discouraged from messing around in the kitchen. You could use any ingredients you found, any time day or night, and make anything in the whole wide world, as long as you cleaned up your mess. This meant that most of us made peanut butter and jelly sandwiches or had an extra helping of ice cream. But if you wanted to scramble eggs, or grill a cheese sandwich, you were certainly welcome.

With a little help from one of the cooks we made a big sheet cake. It was two feet across and we put it on a piece of plywood wrapped in tin foil. We covered it with pink frosting, the official color of the Women's Club. I carefully wrote the note on the top in chocolate icing.

"Nice job," Billy said. "Who wouldn't want a piece of cake like this?"

"Why are we giving them a cake?" I asked.

"Why not? It's just another part of the social experiment."

Exactly five days after Cal found the purse under the bus stop bench, on Friday at 12:30 in the afternoon, wearing our purple Hallboy caps, the three of us hid behind an old Dodge Dart across the P.O.P. from the great house which held the No Palms Women's Club.

"Okay," says Billy. "Walk up there. Like you've done it a thousand times before."

Cal grimaced. With the pink purse tucked under his arm like a football, he lifted the cake carefully, and eased across the street, through the gate in the picket fence, over the walkway, up the steps onto the great wraparound porch. He steadied himself directly in front of the tall pink door and pressed the bell. Then he knocked with the toe of his shoe. We could hear it crisply across the street where we huddled.

The door opened slowly and a little old lady peered out. "Hi lady," he says, loudly enough so we could hear him across the street. "We're returning this purse we found. And here's a cake just for good measure."

The old lady clearly thought she was being spoofed. She stepped backwards, her hand coming up to cover her mouth. Then, collecting herself, "Here, let me help you." And she reached for Betty's lost purse and pulled it quickly from underneath Cal's armpit. She quickly took it inside the door, then reached for the plywood and lifted the cake off

Cal's arms. I did not hear her say thank you. Cal tipped his cap, and said, "Have a nice day, lady." Then he turned and walked back across the porch down the steps, and slowly towards the street. He had a big wide goofy smile across his face.

The lady stood on the porch watching, the big pink cake in her hands. Two other members of the Club joined her on the porch. We could hear their little old lady steps on the wooden boards. When Cal got close to the Dodge Dart where we were hiding, he turned around and gave them a friendly wave. They stepped back inside and slammed the door.

That was it. I don't know what we expected to see, but nothing happened. We figured that the old bats were peeking through the curtains, watching for activity, so we stayed crouched for 15 minutes. When Billy announced the coast was clear we sprinted away, back to the Hall.

*****

None of us had any idea what might happen next. We'd have probably been happy to have heard nothing at all from the Women's Club. Not a peep. No thanks whatsoever. Because that would've confirmed our worst suspicions about Betty Battle and her ilk: more verification that she was the selfish vile old bat we'd long imagined. She'd worn our label of loathing for years, sneering and scowling every time a Hallboy got within a block of her or their clubhouse.

Five days after returning the purse with the extra money, we'd still heard absolutely nothing. We'd increased their booze money, but in return, there was only silence. In our hearts, we'd expected Betty to fire right back. After all, in the past she'd never let any sneaky Hallboy orphans outsmart her.

But the silence was killing us, especially Billy.

"We ain't gonna just sit here while that old hag does nothing. She can't take that extra money and not say anything. Not even a thank you? We could've kept it all. Even Betty has to acknowledge some good Samaritans."

"Maybe she doesn't know there's extra money."

"Of course she does. She knows every bill in that envelope. Trust me. Betty Battle knows whether she has a thin dime or a thick one."

So Billy the Brain took the next step. "C'mon. Let's go."

"Where?"

"Art room."

Billy let us to the Hall's art room. Specifically, to the graphics table. "We're gonna make a sign."

Billy cut and pasted. After 30 minutes we stood back and pondered his handiwork.

REWARD

<u>LOST PURSE</u>

Return it to Betty Battle

$75 Reward paid for Full Recovery

No Questions Asked

"There," says Billy. "We're gonna plaster them all over town. We'll make that old crab come out of her shell."

"Um, Billy? Isn't *she* the one who supposed to post the reward sign?"

"Well, sure. But this is just part of the social experiment."

"But she already has the money back. Aren't you supposed to post a reward sign *before* the lost object is recovered?"

"Yes, doofusses," Billy said with exasperation. "If we're ever gonna get her attention, and if we're ever gonna get *acknowledged* for being such good Hallboys, we gotta jangle her nerves a little bit."

We printed off a whole mess of signs and plastered them up and down the P.O.P., on lamp poles, storefronts, parking meters and trees. We set them out especially thick around the Women's Club.

"You know what, Brain? I don't think it's gonna work. Betty will only accuse us of trying to shake her down. She's just gonna say we're a bunch of skunks."

"Then that's just part of the experiment."

"Don't you think you're taking this experimentation a little too far?" Cal said. "After all, it's not like you're a scientist or anything."

"Of course I'm a scientist," Billy replied. "And Betty is our lab rat. We're gonna see what she's made of."

We had no doubt that Betty Battle received the money back. We also had no doubt she saw the <u>Reward</u> signs posted up and down the P.O.P. They were everywhere. Yet a week later we hadn't heard a thing. Two weeks later, nada. And three full weeks after we returned the purse, we hadn't heard a chirp out of Betty Battle. No friendly call, no visit, no thank you card came in the mail.

As this time passed the incident was almost forgotten. I'm happy to say that thoughts of Betty Battle faded from the front of our minds, replaced by dozens and dozens of other things in our Hallboy lives. Until one evening at supper time Billy smacked his palm on the dining table. "Hey! We never heard anything back about the purse! The old bags never said a single word. Nothing!"

"That," I said, "is what's known as a *thankless task*."

"It's also a damn good deed gone down the drain," Cal added.

"No reward. No note of thanks. Damn!" says Billy.

"Did you really think that Betty would humble herself to some Hallboys?"

Billy shook his head. "I kept telling you guys. I didn't know what to think. I was just trying to be, well, *provocative.*"

"Maybe you provoked her right into silence."

"I guess so. But darn. All we wanted was, you know, to be *acknowledged.*"

That's when the proctor came up and handed me a small folded note. From the Office. I read it. "Crap. The Head of the Hall wants to see us in his office. Right now." This wasn't necessarily bad news. You were always being called into the Office for administrative stuff, paperwork, reminders about a dental appointment, or it was your turn to get new shoes. Besides, we hadn't done anything recently to get into any trouble.

We cleared our plates and trays and marched over to see the Head of the Hall. He motioned us in and quickly sized us up. "Chip, tuck in your shirt. Billy, smooth out that hair. We have guests."

"Guests?"

"Yes. Let's go."

"Where?"

"Out front."

He led us through the Parlor and out the big purple doors, to the front steps.

The steps. That made sense. Because at the bottom of the steps, in the driveway, was a woman and a young girl. The young girl sat in a wheelchair. In those days at Boys Hall, the only way to get a wheelchair inside was to go through the back of the kitchen. You couldn't get a wheelchair up the front steps of Boys Hall.

"Men," says the Head of the Hall. "This is Mrs. Gonzales and her daughter Diana." You didn't see a lot of little girls at Boys Hall. Especially using wheelchairs.

We knew our manners and we moved down the steps. Mrs. Gonzales came forward, big smile on her face. Diana was about our age. She spun her chair and wheeled over. "Are these the boys? Are these the ones who helped?"

Billy and Cal looked at each other. We all looked at Mrs. Gonzales and Diana. The Head of the Hall said nothing, he merely stood there with folded arms. I saw it first.

There it was, plain as day. Printed clearly on a portion of the wheelchair frame: BINGO 101. Billy and Cal saw it too. They looked like they got slapped by a stingray.

"We so much wanted to thank you boys," Mrs. Gonzalez says. "From the bottoms of our hearts. When Betty Battle and the Women's Club set out to buy Diana a new wheelchair, we were so hopeful. She'd outgrown her old one. These chairs are so expensive. The BINGO costs about $1800. The good ladies at the Club raised some money, but they came up short. When Betty called us and told us about the shortfall, we were so disappointed. Until you boys made up the difference. Our prayers were answered. You pushed us over the top. Your contribution, your generosity! You boys are wonderful. So selfless. And look at this beautiful chair. You've truly changed our lives. Thank you."

Stunned, we watched as Diana wheeled herself around the Boys Hall driveway. What a happy kid. Her smile gave us all the thanks we needed.

A few minutes later we walked back to our rooms, in silence. Cal spoke first. "So, Billy. Our social experiment. Now that it's over, would you say that it was a failure, or a success?"

Bill stared at the tray of brownies that Mrs. Gonzales had given us. "We did get acknowledged after all," Billy said softly.

"Can you feel happy and ashamed at the same time?" I asked.

Billy nodded. "Yes you can. I feel both."

I felt both ways too. I felt the happiness first. Happy that we'd helped Diana get a new wheelchair. But just two minutes later, that feeling was gone. It was sort of a bummer. We walked back to our rooms in silence. Betty Battle had put one over on us. We were not elated.

"Billy," I said. "Next time we work on a social experiment, let's think it through a little better first. This one backfired."

"It didn't exactly backfire," Billy said. "After all, that girl got a new wheelchair. If it wasn't for us..."

"And we did get recognized," Cal added. "A big plate of brownies, a nice thank you card, and even a visit."

"Then why aren't we happier?" I asked.

"I dunno. Cause sometimes experiments don't come out like you expect."

*****

Michael Daswick
Scottsdale, Arizona
July, 2014

THE FISHING POLE

1970.

No Palms, California

A fishing pole hangs over the fireplace in the grand Parlor of Boys Hall in No Palms. It's old, weathered, a little bent. The Hall encouraged us to fish as much as we liked, so any Hallboy could borrow the pole at any time. Over the years hundreds of Hallboys had wet a line from the No Palms pier. And while there's nothing particularly special about the old pole over the mantle of the fireplace, almost every Hallboy knew how it came to rest in such a ceremonial spot.

One day we took Mr. Moldyman's bike. He was our history teacher at Boys Hall. It was a Saturday and a bunch of us sixth graders had OPPs: Off Property Passes. Me, Cal, Billy the Brian. The Hall was happy to see kids go off property as long as we wore our purple caps, which were required outside the gates. It was a boring kind of day and as we headed to town we saw Mr. Moldyman's bike parked in the rack. I took the bike. Actually, I borrowed it. After all, I truly expected to return it later that day.

I rode the bike while Cal and Billy walked alongside, the two miles down the Pacific Ocean Parkway to downtown. In those days, No Palms still had a bit of charm. Shops were still doing business, the pier and Seaside Park were active, and beachgoers came from all around to spend the day. Me and Billy and Cal stopped at El Burger Bucket and bought a shake to share three ways. Then we went out onto the pier where, as usual, there were a few old guys fishing. We found an abandoned fishing pole laying on the deck. It was crapped up, worn and rusty. As Billy picked it up the broken line drifted on the breeze.

Billy had an idea: "Let's tie the bike to the fishing line and give it a good push."

"You're nuts."

"Sure!" Billy says. "Chip, knot the line around the frame. Tie it on really strong. We'll do a ghost rider. Just for fun."

We opened the gate in the railing at the end of the pier, between the two red lights. Cal held the pole while I aimed the tires, took a running start, and sent Mr. Moldyman's bike sailing off into the green Pacific, line zinging out of the reel. The bike zipped straight off, wheels spinning, before it dove in. I remember a nice splash, a rise of bubbles, and Mr. Moldyman's bike sunk out of view.

Cal reeled it back up. It broke clear of the water next to a crusty pier piling. Cal reeled it all the way up to the deck where we lifted it and set it down on the planks. "Let's try it again. But this time we'll go faster!" We backed way up, set the wheels straight, ran as fast as we could and let her fly. The bike arched nicely, handlebars holding straight, then dove into the ocean a second time.

"Cool!"

Cal reeled. Again, the bike broke the surface next to the piling. Cal laughed as he reeled it to within five or six feet of the deck of the pier.

Then the line snapped.

We watched mournfully as the bike tipped, then splashed in that dark green water. I had an awful feeling as it sunk into the ocean, right next to the piling. "Rat crap," Cal said, dropping the pole. He and Billy ran for it. I walked back to Boys Hall alone, carrying the fishing pole. I went straight to Mr. Moldyman's office and knocked. I handed him the pole with the broken trailing line.

"What's this?"

"Your bicycle was on the end of this line."

He stared at me. "Chip, where's my bicycle now?"

"Off the end of the pier. At the bottom of the ocean."

I thought I was gonna get a thrashing. Wrinkles formed on Mr. Moldyman's forehead, along with a look of profound sadness. Slowly. I watched his eyes travel from one end of that fishing pole to the other, from the handle to the tip. He snuffled and he shuddered. Then, to my great surprise, a big tear came sliding down his cheek. It moved slowly, leaving a little trail. Then I started to cry as well and in a minute my shame was expressed in a fit of sobbing, my hands squeaking my cheeks. Mr. Moldyman came around his desk and hugged me.

When we stopped crying, he asked me some questions.

"Chip, did you do this alone?"

"Yes I did," I told him. "Sir."

"All by yourself?"

"Yes."

He studied me. "Chip. Are you lying to protect your Hallboy pals?"

"Yes."

"Is it honorable to protect your pals, even if it makes you a liar?"

I stared at him. "I'm not sure."

"Chip. Is it still honorable to protect a friend, even when it involves a dishonorable act to do so?"

I was so confused. "I hope so," I told him. And I started to cry again.

Mr. Moldyman patted the back of my head and pointed to a chair. I sat. He handed me a Kleenex.

Two minutes later he says to me, "Listen to these three punishments. You may choose the one you want."

I nodded.

"You can come to my house on weekends and do my yard-work for the next three months." He saw me gulp. "Or, you can wash dishes and trays in the dining hall, every lunch and dinner, for the next three months." I wiped my nose. "Or, you can make a sign. A large sign. The sign will read, *"I am a bike thief. I stole from my friend."* You would wear this sign around your neck and sit on a bench on the boardwalk, at the foot of the pier. You would do this for 15 afternoons, four hours at a time."

He sat in his desk chair and said, "So, Chip. Which one will you choose?"

I knew the answer. It was easy. "I'll do all three."

He stared at me without expression. Finally he said, "Okay. And here's number four. Your Hall allowance will be suspended for three months as well."

*****

The yardwork at Mr. Moldyman's house was not awful. In fact, I rather enjoyed it.

Dish duty was tolerable.

The sign. This was the Boys Hall version of a public flogging. Stigma. I made a sign with big red letters which bore the exact words dictated by Mr. Moldyman. I hung it around my neck with a shoelace and went downtown to where the boardwalk and the pier come together. I sat on a bench covered in sea-gull poop with my sign and purple Boys Hall cap. On my first day, it was hot out there. Other Hallboys snickered. An old lady from the No Palms Women's Club came by. She stopped and glared, giving me the stink-eye. "You're *despicable*," she snorted, and doddled away. Expected, but still humiliating. Passers-by. Ocean waves behind me. And I got sunburned.

The next day I bought a milk shake at El Burger Bucket before I sat down on my bench. Another old lady stopped and stared. "*Shame* on you Hallboys," she hissed. I drank my shake and kept it close to me on the bench, near my leg, where the gulls couldn't get to it.

About an hour passed. Tourists strolled through No Palms in those days. A stranger walked up, stopped, and read my sign. He had a kind face and I detected a hint of sympathy. He reached into his pocket and dropped a dollar bill into my shake. This was a surprise. He went on his way. I dipped into my cup, fished out the dollar, wiped it clean and dry. An hour later some guy dropped in 50 cents. By the end of the day I had over six dollars.

The next time I brought an empty cup. I did nothing differently, I spoke not a word. Except thank you. I made $8.55 on the second day. After six weeks I had over $200. This was much better than a Boys Hall allowance.

*****

I did my bench duty, with my sign and cup. I'd later learn that Mr. Moldyman had been watching me from time to time, from a ways up the P.O.P., to make sure I was doing my time. Unknown to me, he saw people putting coins in my cup.

I was at Mr. Moldyman's house the next Sunday, raking leaves. I thought I was pretty sly. "Mr. Moldyman?" I asked.

"Yes, Chip?"

"How much does a new bike cost?"

"A decent three-speed is about a hundred dollars."

Meanwhile, Billy the Brain was smart and he fashioned a grappling hook in the Hall's mechanical shop. Cal could swim real well and one day they went down to the pier. Cal took the hook and rope and dove into the water, right next to the piling. He went all the way to the bottom and snagged the bike. They tugged it up, hand over hand. It was much rustier than before. Billy and Cal took their allowance and bought rust remover and oil and a new chain and cleaned up the bike. They painted it purple. One evening they left it in Mr. Moldyman's classroom with a note: *We're sorry about your bike. Signed, Hallboy X and Hallboy Z.*"

I bought Mr. Moldyman a new three-speed. He was grateful. Then he surprised me. He asked, "Chip...you got any extra money from your milkshake cup?"

"Huh?"

"Yes. Money from your milkshake cup."

"Uh....yeah."

"Do you think it's fair that you should keep it?"

"Well, no. Not exactly. But people gave it to me."

"Well, yes they did. But what about this. Let's fix up this old fishing pole. Hallboys can use it when they want to fish."

So we bought a new reel and line. We took off the rust. We retied the guides and spiffed it up. We made a little project out of it and Mr. Moldyman loved that fishing pole. We carried it out to the front lawn and took turns casting. It was fun. When we were done he placed it above the fireplace in the Parlor for all to admire.

Kids take the pole out fishing all the time and it's especially coveted during the annual Boys Hall Fishing Derby, where it's deemed very lucky. When not in use on the pier it hangs over the fireplace in the Parlor, to this day. My *"I am a bike thief"* sign hangs there too.

*****

Michael Daswick
Scottsdale, 2015

CHIP ROCK and the ANCIENT LIGHTHOUSE

The crumbling ruin of the ancient lighthouse sits on the very top of the cliffs which surround No Palms cove. High above the crashing ocean water, at the edge of the cliffs which fall straight into the sea, the old stone turret stands sentinel over the blue Pacific. Some of the blocks are as large as washing machines, held fast through the years by a mighty mortar and a chalky mantle of seagull poop. For over 200 years, it's withstood the lashing rains, gales, the clouds of fog, winter's gloom and summers sparkling sunlight. It has also withstood the company of a thousand Hallboys who, over the years, used the ancient lighthouse as a fort, a rendezvous, a signal point, climbing tower, picnic spot, campground, resting place and fire-pit backdrop. Many other people from No Palms and along the coast have come to the lighthouse ruin for parties, eons of stunning sunsets, and an array of nighttime endeavors.

Sailors off the SoCal coast have always seen these cliffs from miles offshore, the headlands tall and prominent along the coast. Standing next to the lighthouse, you can look down on the ocean, the No Palms pier, our crappy cannery, and town itself. If you stand on the pier, looking back towards town, the old walled beach ends and the cove begins; the land rises quickly behind the soaring cliffs which loom hundreds of feet above the thumping waves. And high atop the cliffs, there it is: the old thumb of the lighthouse.

It's believed the ancient lighthouse was built in the late 1700s. Originally it stood over 50 feet tall and its beacon, they say, was easily seen clear across the channel to Catalina Island, and by mariners even 50 miles away. Local historians say the lighthouse served many functions: navigation; a warning to steer clear of the cliffs in the fog; fishermen used it to reference their favorite spots at sea. It was also useful for naval logistics in the military days. Long before there ever was a pier, that lighthouse was the signature landmark of our little town.

*****

Almost every Hallboy in the No Palms Boys Hall has no family. We never heard much talk about anybody's mom or dad or grandparents. Consequently, the Hall worked hard to provide Hallboys with as meaningful a past as possible. The Hall made every attempt to give us a history, a foundation. The Hall wove the fabric of an ancestry and tried damn hard to craft a legacy so that each of us would have something to cling to. During my years at the Hall, the person most responsible for imparting this sense of a past was our history teacher, Mr. Moldyman. I have to say that I found Mr. Moldyman's classes to be fascinating. History was much better than, say, math. Science was not very colorful beyond the age of the dinosaurs. English still meant spelling and vocabulary and memorizing a million rules of grammar. Spanish? None of us ever expected to get to Spain. And nobody ever told us that they spoke Spanish in Mexico.

I liked Mr. Moldyman's history classes. We learned all about the Hall itself, how it was founded, how it grew as a local institution. The Hall preserved its own records in great detail. There was even a position for an older boy known as Hall Historian. Little did I know back in 6th grade, but when I was in high school and before I aged out, I'd assume this position: Chip Rock -- Hall Historian. Reporter, chronicler, record keeper, commentator. In any case, our history teacher Mr. Moldyman taught us everything about the Hall. After all, it was our home.

He also taught us general California history, about the missions and the gold rush and the hapless pioneers who crossed Donner Pass in the winter and Death Valley in the summer. And finally, to cement our sense of legacy and pride, we learned all about the *local* history of No Palms itself, from its birth as a fruit orchard or prune farm or something, to its growth, fueled by the sardine cannery next to the pier.

One week as we sat in history class, Mr. Moldyman blew his nose and cleared his throat and told us the story behind the ancient lighthouse. He paced back and forth across the front of the classroom, upstairs in the main building, his dusty black wing-tips clomping on the wooden floor. "All you boys have been to the top of the cliffs," he said. "You climbed up there many times, I suppose. But did you know those cliff-tops were used by a certain group *long before* there ever was a lighthouse?"

"Huh?"

"In fact, *legend* has it that our cliffs were used by a certain group of people way back in the 1600s. *Almost 400 years ago.* Does anyone know who used our cliffs first? Almost 400 years ago?"

Billy the Brain always knew answers like this. "Injuns," Billy declared.

"No," Mr. Moldyman said.

While we were racking our brains, Mr. Moldyman continued. "I'll tell you who. I'll tell you who used those cliffs first. It was the *Pirates.*"

*****

One of the Hall's annual events was the spring camp out on the end of the No Palms pier during the April full moon. This was a warm-up of sorts for the great Fishing Derby in August. However, unlike the Derby where the entire Hall was invited, only nine select Hallboys were awarded the opportunity to camp out in April. Which Hallboys got to camp? The ones who won the Boys Hall spelling bee.

Over the years the Boys Hall spelling bee was not our most popular competition. In fact, boys routinely and intentionally misspelled easy words so they could sit back down and doodle or take a nap. The Head of the Hall grew weary of this non-participation so during our 6th grade year he *incentivized* the bee: the top three finishers would be allowed to camp out on the end of the pier on the night of April's full moon. Each winner could invite two pals to join him. Nine campers in all. Given that a night off Hall property was almost completely unheard of, the spelling bee captured our attention.

Kids tried hard. Hallboys stayed up late to study, quizzing each other in advance. The bee was held in the grand Parlor. Mr. Moldyman presided. I could spell reasonably well and I found myself advancing through the rounds. Billy the Brain cussed and fell out when he spelled *pier*, 'p-e-i-r'. Cal bit the dust when, with fists clenched, he spelled *truant* with two many u's. I sewed up third place when I guessed right on *mackerel.* I knew I was a camper. Johnny the Atom took second. That was cool. Johnny was part of our group.

Then there was Ling Ling, the Chinese kid. His nickname was Ping Pong. He was short and almost frail and he wasn't exactly a part of our little group. Billy called him a weenie because he was so sensitive about little stuff, but he had a mind like a camera. He advanced through the rounds and as the bee wore down to the harder words, we were all thinking the same thing: it would be nice not to have to camp with

Ling Ling. Each of us felt a spark of optimistic when Mr. Moldyman smirked and gave Ping Pong the word, *enchilada.* "Enchilada," Ping Pong repeated, and then he paused to swallow. Billy elbowed me. Ping Pong stared at Billy and spelled the word out as fast as could be. It only took him about half a second. Then he added, looking directly at Billy the Brain, "One of my favorite things to eat is … an enchilada." Billy rolled his eyes. His spelling was correct, of course, and that little geek won the bee. I chose my buddies Cal and Billy to join me on the camp out. The full moon would be on a Saturday night, only two weeks away.

*****

"Pirates?" asked Cal. "We had pirates in No Palms?"

"Yep. If you believe the legends, yes we did," answered Mr. Moldyman as he clomped across the wooden floor. "I've read that pirates used our very beach frequently between 1620 and 1650." Cal and I looked at each other from our position in the back of the history classroom. We leaned forward, ears tuned to every word. "They used what little shelter the No Palms cove offered to anchor their ships, to replenish water, come ashore to hunt for game, or just to feel their feet standing on solid ground." Mr. Moldyman cast an eye to the back of his class and saw, for once, all of us were completely entranced with concentration. Then he continued, "They also came ashore. Do you know why?"

"Why??"

"To lay in wait."

The room fell silent. "To lay and wait for what?" asks Billy the Brain.

"Well. For other ships, of course," Mr. Moldyman replied, very matter of fact.

"You mean so they could sink 'em?" asked Cal.

"No. They wouldn't want to sink them. Rather, they would've wanted to *plunder* them."

"Plunder?"

"Yes. To rob them. Steal their stuff. Remember….any boats in these waters way back then were trading vessels. In those days the pirates would take their goods." Mr. Moldyman had our attention. This was certainly way better than grammar. "The pirates had the fastest ships. Oftentimes there were cannons on deck. There wasn't exactly a Coast Guard back then. These pirates disguised their ships to look like traders or even peaceful fishing boats." He clomped along the floor, footsteps ringing out. "But in actual fact," he stopped: "these pirates were *deadly*."

The classroom remained silent for several moments. Then, Billy the Brain spoke out. "How do you know so much about these pirates?"

Mr. Moldyman flashed a quick glance at Billy. "As with any legend," he started walking again, slower now. "As with any legend, there are *sources* which historians read. In this case, the best sources that we have are the actual *logbooks* from various friendly merchant vessels which sailed these waters. These logs, you know, were kept *daily* with great diligence and attention to detail. Remember. This was the age of exploration. Posting records and mapping your way was a critical element for any sea-man. In such an age of discovery, it was the captain and the pilot's job to record routes, headings, all aspects of geography, currents, weather, even the fish they caught. Their accuracy…" Mr. Moldyman said with the utmost authority, "Their accuracy is not to be questioned."

I accepted this as a very convincing answer.

"Logbooks?" Billy persisted. "What logbooks? Where do they keep these... logbooks?"

Mr. Moldyman was not irritated in the least by Billy's inquisition. "Why Billy, you'll find a *wall-full* of logbooks in the Western Maritime Museum. Down the coast in Long Beach. We'll have to go there one of these days."

Billy the Brain sat back in his chair, glanced around at us, and the look of satisfaction spread across his face. "In any case," Mr. Moldyman continued, "hundreds of years before the lighthouse was ever built, can anyone guess what the pirates used to do on the tops of our cliffs?"

Every Hallboy in history class dearly wanted to be the kid to call out the correct answer. "The pirates captured the captains of the trading ships," says Johnny the Atom. "They took over the ships right off the cliffs and marched them up to the tops where they pushed them over and fed 'em to the sharks."

Many of us held our breath. Mr. Moldyman paused. "There's no evidence of that type of behavior," he said factually. "However, there is no doubt that these pirates were cruel and ruthless characters."

"EEEEEeeeeeeeeee.....ker-PLOOOSH!" says Cal, mimicking the sound of a sea captain falling off the cliffs, through the air, splashing into the sea.

"Did the pirates camp up there?" asks Ling Ling.

"Maybe."

"Did they have sword fights?" asked a Hallboy.

"Sure. Anyone could challenge the Captain's leadership at any time."

"Dang."

"But do you men know what the pirates would actually do up on the top of those cliffs?"

"What? What!"

"They'd light enormous signal fires."

"I knew it!" shouts Billy.

"WOW! How come?"

"To signal other pirate ships, of course. Our cliffs are the highest point along the coast for many many many miles. And from our cove, the pirates would signal other ships to let them know when they were here in port, at anchor. They'd no doubt meet up and exchange information.

"There's still a fire pit up there now," I called out.

"Yes, Chip, there is. Of course, the one there today is from kids and people who go up there at night, have a party, make a bonfire."

"Yeah," says Billy the Brain. "And they drink a lot of beer up there."

"But the idea is the same," Mr. Moldyman said. "The pirates made an enormous fire ring, stoked up a big bonfire, and let it be seen far out to sea for many a mile."

This, we acknowledged, was a fabulous tale. We looked at each other and back at Mr. Moldyman with admiration. "That's right, boys. The pirates would gather, and trade their plunder with other pirates. We had ruthless pirates right here in No Palms."

*****

Our happy little Hallboy gang of nine 6th graders began preparations for pier camping immediately. The Hall had two old military canvas tents which we carried from the garage. We spread them out on the great lawn for freshening and afterwards, proudly set them up in front of the Hall. When we staked down the corners and raised the center poles, lifting the tents into their full upright form, other Hallboys marveled in admiration. We assembled our overnight bags, bedrolls, the purple Hall flag, towels, chairs, ice chest, flashlights, and plenty of eats. Three nights before Saturday, we stared at the moon, which was fast growing full. We were ready to go.

*****

In history class Mr. Moldyman moved along from pirate talk and was lecturing about the early California explorers. He tacked up a big map which traced the routes traveled by the famous great names: Balboa, Cabrillo, and Sir Francis Drake.

He stopped his pacing and posed a question to the class: "Who was the first person, or who were the first people, to see the Pacific Ocean? Was it Balboa, as history always says? Or the Indians? Or was it….the Chinese?"

Ling Ling was the sole Chinese kid at the Hall. We had more nicknames for Ling Ling than perhaps any other kid, but Ping Pong was the name that stuck. "Who saw the Pacific Ocean first?" repeated Mr. Moldyman.

"It musta been the Indians," says Cal. "Because they were here before the explorers."

"Was it the Indians?" Mr. Moldyman asked the class.

"Balboa," says Billy the Brain. "He climbed up a hill in Panama and when he got to the top he looked over to the other side. Bingo! There was the Pacific."

"Was it Balboa?"

We all looked at Mr. Moldyman with great suspense. He says, "It can be argued that either Balboa or the Indians saw it first. However, most historians today would say, most will tell you, the first people to really see the Pacific stood on the *other* side of the world. They saw the other side of the Pacific. Thousands of years before anyone else. It was the *Chinese!*"

Ping Pong looked up and smiled. He sat tall in his chair, looking around at the rest of us, his body swelling with pride.

"No way!" shouts Johnny the Atom, looking directly at Ping Pong. "No way the Chinamen saw it first."

"Did too," counters Ping Pong.

"Did not!"

"Did too! We saw it before anyone. And then we built the Great Wall!"

"Big deal. A stupid *wall*."

"It is a big deal."

"It's just a stupid wall!"

"It's not just a stupid wall. You can see it from the *moon!*"

"How do you know? You ain't never been to the moon."

"Have so."

"Have not!"

"Have so!"

"Have not!"

"Okay boys, okay. Scholars are learning that the Chinese were much more aggressive sailors than previously thought. They likely saw their side of the Pacific hundreds of years before anyone from Europe. Either way, historians pretty much agree that besides the Chinese or Indians or anyone else, the first *European* to see our Pacific Ocean was indeed Balboa. He was the first *Westerner* to see it." Johnny the Atom looked over at Ping Pong and stuck out his tongue. "Boys. What do you think was the very first thing that Balboa and his men *said* when they first saw the Pacific? What did they say when they first laid eyes on the great new ocean?"

We all sat still, scrambling our brains for a good answer.

"It sure is *big*!" I said. Mr. Moldyman nodded.

"Balboa said, 'I wonder what's on the other side'," says Billy the Brain. More nods.

Then Cal answered, "They said, 'Wow! Let's go for a swim'!"

*****

The Saturday morning of the April full moon saw us up before sunrise assembling our camping gear out on the great lawn. Sergeant Bernie Butterbar agreed to be our chaperone, the adult who'd camp with us. Sergeant Butterbar was the police chief of No Palms, but Hallboys simply knew him as our baseball coach. He was a nice guy who taught sportsmanship and let us play hard and he gave us lots of space and, despite his position as the town cop, he was no stickler for the rules as far as the Hallboys were concerned. We loaded up the two police cars, put on our purple Hallboy caps, and caught a ride downtown. We proudly unloaded our stuff on the boardwalk at the foot of the pier, near the old stinking cannery. Cal and I lugged the first tent down to the end of the pier, Billy and Johnny hauled the second. We deposited everything next to the two blinking red lights on the very end rail. It was a bright sunny April day and Cal, who loved to watch the waves and the tides, leaned back on the railing as ocean swells rolled beneath us. "This is gonna be great," says Cal. "This is gonna be great!"

We spread out the tents side by side and Coach Butterbar helped us tie down the corners with rope and pull everything tight. We lifted the center-poles straight up and stood back to admire our work. "How cool is this?" asked the Atom. A few old-timers -- out fishing – gave us the thumbs up. We opened our bedrolls and laid out our snacks. "Hey,

Coach," I yelled to Sergeant Butterbar. "You gonna sleep in a tent with us?"

"No way," says Coach. "I don't wanna be in there with you screwballs. I wanna get some rest... I brought my own tent." We helped Coach Butterbar set up his little one-man pup tent a short distance away. Then he said, "You guys stay here, I'm gonna run and get my barbeque and a bag of coals. We'll cook-out tonight."

"Bitchen," says Johnny the Atom.

Ping Pong's supplies were neatly arranged by the side of his bedroll. Billy nudged the bag of pretzels and box of crackers with his sneaker and stared longingly at Ping Pong's jar of peanut butter. "Why didn't I think of that?" Billy asked me. Then, "Hey PP. I'll trade you some M & Ms for a sleeve of crackers and a big lump of peanut butter."

"That's a lousy trade for me," says Ping Pong.

"Then M & Ms and two Slim Jims."

"Forget it, Billy. I don't wanna trade."

"Suit yourself. But if you don't share that peanut butter I'm just gonna steal it from you."

*****

We lazed the day away on the pier. Coach Butterbar fired up the grill and cooked hot dogs for lunch. He promised burgers for dinner. We swam in the ocean, doing cannonballs and jack-knives off the end of the pier. We looked in the fishermen's buckets and Billy spotted a red starfish on one of the pilings. We proudly hoisted the purple Boys Hall flag. Ping Pong got a splinter in his foot from one of the crappy old planks and Billy told him, "You can dig it out with my pocket knife if you give me some peanut butter."

"Fine. And by the way, Brain, I was gonna give you some anyways."

By the middle of the afternoon every miserable mooching seagull on the coast knew we were there and Cal said he should have remembered to bring his slingshot. Otherwise, we were content and we leaned back on the railing, our backs to the sea. We gazed in towards town at the string of cruddy shops, the old cannery building, the trees in Seaside Park. The cove curved around to the left side of the pier, with the enormous cliffs behind. Up on top, far in the distance, we could make out the ruin of the ancient lighthouse.

"Who wants to hike to the top of the cliffs and throw rocks?" asks Johnny.

"Not me," says Billy. "I'm too lazy. It's too hot. I ain't climbing that stinking hill."

"C'mon! Let's go," Johnny says.

"You go yourself," says Cal. "It's too far. But I'll go to the Little Store for some bubble gum." So we dashed off to the Little Store and raided the candy counter. We bought sodas and chips, then piddled around on the pier and bugged Coach Butterbar for a while. The full moon appeared over the low hills behind No Palms and as the sun drifted lower Coach fired up the barbeque again for dinner. We stood around the coals while Coach flipped the meat and the burgers flamed and sizzled and more dumb gulls swooped around. Everybody had seconds as a few puffy clouds drifted out of the south. Cal noted that the tide was coming in and that the swells were stronger. A breeze picked up. The few lonely fishermen reeled up for the day and snapped their tackle boxes shut. We couldn't wait for the sun to set – when we'd be all alone out on the end of the pier.

"Test your flashlights," says Coach. Dinner over, he doused the barbeque. "I'm going in my tent to read. You boys stay outa trouble and try not to bug me unless someone falls off the pier and drowns." We sat around carving our names into the railings with Billy's pocket knife. With dusk upon us Billy looked up and says, "Dudes! Look! Here comes Mr. Moldyman!"

*****

Sure enough, our history teacher Mr. Moldyman was making his way down the pier, old shoes clomping on the wooden planks.

"Boys. Boys!" he calls out cheerily. "Wow. Look at those tents! What a camp! You guys got it made out here." Coach stuck his head out his pup tent as Mr. Moldyman held up a box. "Hallboys! Look what I found in the kitchen. Ice cream sandwiches! Mr. Moldyman proudly displayed an entire case of the treats. "There's plenty enough....how does *three* for each of you sound!"

"Golly, Mr. Moldyman," says Cal. "You're the greatest!" We tore in-to the ice cream like barracudas and Mr. Moldyman was wonderful. He kept saying, "Take another one, you've only had two. Take more." We sat around with the gulls scavenging and screeching. The moon rose higher and more clouds piled overhead as the sun slid down and finally rested on the lip of the sea. Mr. Moldyman told us stories about the Hall and about No Palms and he was funny and entertaining and then he raised his arm and pointed to the top of the cliffs and says, "Hey boys, see the ancient lighthouse? Way up there? 400 years ago, that was the pirates' favorite spot."

"Yeah," says Johnny the Atom. "That was their lookout where they set their signal fires."

"That's exactly correct. But you boys know what else?" He paused. Oh no, thinks I. Here comes the dramatic side of Mr. Moldyman. "You know what else the legends say?" I looked at Billy. Mr. Moldyman's finger remained trained on the old lighthouse. "*Treasure.* Pirate treasure. Legend has it the pirates buried their treasure *somewhere* up on those cliff-tops. Very near to where the old lighthouse now stands."

"Buried treasure?" whispers Billy the Brain. "You never told us that before. The pirates buried their treasure *here*? In cruddy old No Palms?"

"Yes sir," says Mr. Moldyman with a confident nod. "Of course, No Palms wasn't here 400 years ago. There were no towns at all way back them. But from everything I've read, they buried their treasure somewhere up there. There's also stories about caves in these cliffs, at the waterline, with underwater grottos where chests of gold were hidden. But for my money, the pirates carried their fortunes up to the high ground. Out of the way. Away from the water."

"Where did the treasure come from?" asks Ping Pong.

"Well, usually, Mexico."

"Mexico?"

"Yes. Spanish *galleons* used to sail up from Mexico. These were the *Conquistadores*. The Spaniards were traders and explorers and they wanted to return to Spain with all the riches of the New World. All the riches they could find. They had in fact found gold in Mexico. And their greed was great. They heard fables and stories about more gold and fabulous wealth in California. So they sailed up from Mexico...searching. They truly thought there'd be more gold waiting for them here. Of course, they didn't think they'd run into *pirates*."

"What happened?"

"Legend says the pirates laid low here in this very cove. With their ships disguised, they looked harmless enough. Of course in those early days there was no navy or harbor patrol or anything like that. When the Spanish sailed by, the pirates plundered ship after ship. They took the Spanish gold."

"Dang," said Johnny.

"Well, the pirates knew the Spanish would return. With bigger boats and more men. To get their gold back. So the pirates hid it. High up on the cliffs. Away from the waves and the tides. They buried it deep deep down in the ground and marked the spot with a stone *cairn*. A cairn is a huge pile of rocks. Then they built other cairns – *false* cairns, false cairns with false shafts and fake entrenchments and sneaky crypts – to *confound* anyone who might try to steal their treasure. The tales say the original cairn built to mark the true location is exactly the spot where the old ancient lighthouse stands today."

We looked at Mr. Moldyman and then up to the cliff tops. Mr. Moldyman clomped back and forth across the wooden pier planks.

"Is the gold still there today?" asks Cal.

Big pause. "That's the million dollar question. Is there buried treasure in No Palms? Well, if you examine all the evidence and if you ask me, I'd say *Yes*. It was never ever found. The treasure is still there today. And I betcha it's right under those huge stones of the ancient lighthouse."

With the setting sun the breeze picked up and the gathering clouds turned gray. "Can't they find it?" Johnny asked. "Can't they dig it up?"

"Oh they've tried. Oh my yes. Treasure hunters. Scavengers. Archeologists. Many many people have searched and searched. Have they ever found it? No one knows for sure, but probably not. It remains lost. Lost gold. The pirates were very clever and they knew their business well. Did the pirates ever return to get their own gold? Or did they return to bury even more? No one knows for sure."

"Wow!"

"But I do know one thing for sure." He paused and his footsteps stopped. "On certain spring and summer nights, on certain nights when there's a full moon…." (Mr. Moldyman looked up into the darkness and stared at the moon.) "….the pirates return. They return to No Palms cove. They come back under the light of the full moon. *They come back to retrieve their gold.*"

"Whoa!" Ping Pong teetered back with a look of shocked amazement.

Johnny the Atom sat speechless.

Cal stared through the dusk at the lighthouse ruin, far away on the cliff tops.

Billy the Brain spat on the planks. "Oh, *Pooh*! Ain't no pirates and ain't no buried treasure. The only thing up there are old rocks and beer cans…."

"I've heard those legends too," booms Sergeant Butterbar, emerging from his pup tent. "I've heard those legends myself. Boys, lemme tell you. I been in this town a long long time. I've been up and down this shoreline, up and down those cliffs. All I can tell you is this. *Categorically.* Your teacher is right. Each and every time there's a full moon around here, weird stuff seems to happen. Strange things happen. I've heard sounds from the clifftops. I've run up there in the middle of the night many times because there were reports of…." Coach Butterbar stopped and gulped. "I've *seen* things on those cliff tops. Pirates? *Buccaneers?* Boys, you'd better believe it."

"Holeee smokes!" says Johnny.

"Yikes," says Ping Pong.

And with that, a cloud passed in front of the full moon and the pier went dark, except of course for the eerie glow from the two red lights on the end. There was a gust of wind and Billy the Brain sunk back and I could tell he'd lost a bit of his bravado. Coach Butterbar disappeared back into his tent. The air felt different and we sat in creepy silence with the *whump* of the waves slamming the base of the cliffs. There was a mysterious phosphorescence to the water but the clouds closed off the last few stars and with nothing but the red glow, we all looked at Cal. After all, Cal was the weather-watcher amongst us. He knew the tides and winds. The breeze ruffled his hair and Cal says, "Hallboys. Have you noticed? The seagulls are all gone. There's gonna be a storm tonight."

*****

When the first raindrops began to fall Billy asked, "Does anyone think we oughta get back to the Hall?"

"No way," says Johnny. "They'd all laugh at us forever. We stick it out. It's just a spring shower. Right, Cal?"

"I think so," says Cal.

"You guys check your lashings," says Mr. Moldyman. "Tighten up the tents. Not sure if it's a spring shower or big thunderstorm, but I'm getting wet. I'll see you in class on Monday. And boys, watch out." He dropped his voice to a whisper. "Watch out for those pirates."

*****

The raindrops grew larger and the wind blew in and we took shelter in our tents, four of us in one, five in the other. Coach Butterbar stuck his head in the flaps and said, "Hang on to your hats, boys. Batten down the hatches!"

"I'm scared of lightning," Ping Pond moaned.

"Ain't nothing to be scared of," Coach answered back. "There's a lightning rod on every pier in the world. There on the corner. Safest place to be in a storm. But I'm getting soaked. See ya!" And with that, Coach zipped himself inside his tent.

We tied the flaps tight from the inside but the rain fell harder and then came sideways and the wind rocked the tent like it was a big cardboard box. "Everyone take a corner," Billy cried out. The four of us inside tent number one manned our corners, holding fast. I felt a big roller go under the pier and the pilings creaked. The entire pier *swayed*. We sat listening to the pelting rain and when leaks appeared and drips fell about us, I dearly wished Coach Butterbar would come join us, with his big flashlight and ride out the storm. But Coach did not budge.

The storm grew. We could hear the Ka-pows of the waves slamming into the cliffs. Each Hallboy cringed as the old pier growled and each creaking grew and the sways turned to lurches. The wind battered the old canvas and Ping Pong wailed from the other tent. Then, without warning, a horrific gust slammed our tent and the center-pole snapped and the tent collapsed on top of us. "Help!" yells Billy. "Get out! Get out!" Heavy wet canvas flattened us and we scrambled to find the flaps and flee.

"We're gonna blow into the water!" "Gimme your flashlight!" "Cut the flaps!" "Coach!" Cal got the flaps open and as wind and rain tore at us, in the glow of the red pier lights, the second tent tore from its anchors, tumbled, and collapsed on our five mates. Ping Pong's wails creased the air, and moments later, nine Hallboys sat in the driving rain, huddled on top of the mangled canvas, corners flapping. We were taking a helluva soaking. Coach Butterbar, secure in his tight little tent, yelled, "Ride it out, boys! Ride it out!"

The first flash of lightning sent shivers through our little group. The thunder that followed made my wet hair tingle and I felt ice cold down the back of my neck. The pier lurched again and again I looked to Cal for strength but he sat in a ball, frozen in fear.

"Let's run for El Bucket!" I yelled.

"I'm too scared!" Johnny answered. The next flash of lightning lit up our hapless little scene: nine drenched boys with purple caps soaked through. We had no jackets. We'd never expected a storm. Another lightning flash and then another. I glanced up and – for a second -- the entire face of the cliff was *illuminated* as the biggest flash yet lit up the cove. A rip of thunder got our attention and everybody looked up just as another peel of lightning flashed.

We all saw it at once. If only for a split second, but it was unmistakable. I know we all saw the same thing because at first, none of us could speak. On the top of the headlands, as lightning flashed, the turret of the ancient lighthouse was easy enough to see. But there was more. Figures. *People.* Then darkness again, until the pitch dark was broken by the next flash.

"Did you see them?" cried Johnny.

I saw it again. More figures. In the instant that lightning comes and goes, we all saw the figures on top of the cliffs. "There's a pack of dudes up there," Cal gasped, horror across his face. We strained our eyes through the driving rain. Flash. There they were again. Then darkness. We sat mesmerized. Another flash. The figures remained, but now they were different. They had *moved.* Stick figures, appearing white against black, like a strobe, only for a moment. The next flash. "They're moving around!"

"He turned."

"Did you see the big hat?"

"Working! In boots!"

"He's bending over a shovel."

"No! It's a pick-axe!"

I saw a jacket flapping and Cal grabbed my arm. I could feel the terror in his squeezing. Thunder bounced off the cliffs and, finally, silence fell. My mind played back what I'd just seen, over and over. There were men atop the cliffs. Moving. Crouching. Was I certain?

The next bolt struck right above us, simultaneous with a deafening thunderclap. This time there was no mistake. We each saw it: the lightning struck straight into the turret of the ancient lighthouse. This was followed by an explosion of flame from the cliff top, a bright red blaze. The figures on the cliff reeled back and fell away into the dark. I heard a distant scream, followed by thunder off the rocks.

The final bolt hit the old pier with a crack that was so close we could *smell* the planks burn. Lightning rod or not, the jolt rattled every timber and every railing down to the old cleats and cables, as if that pier were made of toothpicks. The red pier lights blinked, then went out.

"Coach!"

"Run for it!" Billy was off, with Ping Pong right behind. We all followed, hysterical.

Coach Butterbar shouted, "Wait, boys. It's just a storm!" But we were gone, running off that pier as if fleeing hell itself. We shot through the rain, over the boardwalk and across the P.O.P., heading for the only lights we saw: El Burger Bucket. There we took refuge, gasping, dripping, frantic.

There wasn't a word for several minutes while we panted and groaned.

Finally, I had to ask, "Did you see them? Who saw them? Who saw them up there?"

"I did," says Johnny the Atom.

"Me too."

"It was a whole gang."

"What were they?"

While the rain continued outside we huddled in El Bucket. Ping Pong began to cry. Naturally, I did what was expected from any Hallboy of merit and I put my arm around him and Billy the Brain grabbed his shoulder and Billy says, "It's okay, Ping Pong. It's all okay."

"But Brain…" Ping Pong said through his sobs. "What were they?"

Billy just shook his head. "I dunno, PP. But you were brave as could be, Ping Pong. You are one brave dude."

We found our composure soon enough but there wasn't a lot of conversation. The scare lingered in me. I couldn't get those images out of my mind. We pooled our money and had enough for three fudge sundaes with 9 spoons. Coach Butterbar eventually came looking for us.

"Coach," says Johnny the Atom. "Did you see them?"

"See what?"

"People. On top of the cliffs. During the storm."

Coach Butterbar looked at us. Ping Pong still sniffled. I know that Coach could tell: we were spooked. "People?"

"On the top of the cliffs," Billy said. "They lit up in the lightning. They looked like goons. Or phantoms."

"Did you see them?"

Coach went face to face across the room. "Guys. I gotta tell you. I was scared to death.I never even looked out my tent," he says softly. "What was up there?"

"I dunno, Coach. But it was *weird.*"

Coach looked at us again. He could tell. "You boys are very courageous."

"Coach Butterbar," says Johnny. "Don't tell anyone back at the Hall that we ran. Don't tell 'em that we hid out at the Bucket."

*****

We stayed most of the night in the No Palms police station. The storm passed and Coach awoke us around 5:30 AM so we could get back out to the pier and sleep for an hour. That way we could say we'd camped out.

We packed up all our soggy tents and supplies and returned to the Hall Sunday morning in time for chapel. After that we went to the dining room for Sunday lunch. The nine of us sat around the same table but apart from other Hallboys. Cal whispered, "So. Anybody got any ideas? What the heck happened out there last night?"

"I don't know," says Billy the Brain. "But I wasn't as scared as the rest of you chickens."

"Liar. You were the first to run," says Johnny. "You ran off before Ping Pong."

"Did not."

"Did too."

"We gotta get up to the cliff top," I said. "We gotta go look around. *Something* was up there last night."

"I ain't going back," says Ping Pong.

"I'll go," says Cal.

"We can go today," I says. "On our Sunday free time."

"You gotta come with us, Ping Pong. You're braver than you think."

"Then let's hurry up," says the Atom. "Everybody shut their mouths and eat!"

*****

We grabbed our damp caps and signed out and ran down the P.O.P. to downtown, past the crummy shops and El Burger Bucket, Seaside

Park, the stinking cannery and the pier. We raced up the goat path that led to the top of the cliffs and the ancient lighthouse. With the bright sun out once again and clear skies, there was fear no more in our little band.

We were out of breath before we were halfway up the muddy trail. Almost at the top, Cal says, "You guys smell that smell?"

"Wow," says Billy. "Something is *burning*."

"Or, something *was* burning."

Within 20 yards of the rubble of the old lighthouse, we stopped. The entire southern side of the stone turret was completely charred, an area as large as a garage door.

"It's completely blackened," Brain said.

"You can still smell the fire."

"Look!" says Johnny. "Here's where the lightning hit!"

"Whoa," says Cal. "But what the heck was burning?"

"The *stones* was burning, stupid," says Billy.

"Stones can't burn," Cal answered.

"Oh you bet they can," says Billy. "Anything can burn if it gets hot enough. Stones, rocks, metal. Lightning is *hot*. That's why the lighthouse caught fire."

We crept closer to the ruins. "Sure stinks *funny*," says Johnny.

"That's the electrical smell," says the Brain. "From the electrical charge of the lightning."

"Whoa." We all touched the charred stones.

Then Cal shouts, "Dudes! Look! Boot heels in the mud!"

We ran over. In the muddy earth, clear as day, were the impressions of square boot heels pressed all about the ground. "There! And more here! Over there. They're all around!"

"Look at this one," says Johnny. "Different shoes!"

"Here," says Ping Pong. "Look here. They were....they were....*digging!*" We dashed over.

"Shovel marks! They're all over!"

"They're everywhere."

"They were digging holes."

We spread out across the cliff tops, ignoring the view and the expanse of the Pacific Ocean far below. Instead our eyes were fixed on the mud where boot heels and foot prints and shovel marks were everywhere. We found them all about the lighthouse, all along the entire crest of the cliff. We also found plenty of pits, trenches and holes, freshly dug.

"This is creepy," says Billy.

"It's just nuts!"

"Who was up here? Guys...it was a *gang!*"

"But a gang of what?"

"A gang of pirates?"

"Not exactly pirates," says Cal. "It was a gang of *ghosts!*" We all squirmed, gasping at Cal's words. The G word. The word that none of us had been brave enough to mention up to that point.

"Darn right it was a gang," says Billy. "Ghosts or pirates or whatever they were. But guess what? You know what they were doing? *They were looking for the gold!*"

"The gold?"

"Yeah. The gold that's in the legends. The gold must still be up here."

"No way."

"Yes way," says Billy. "And we're gonna go get us a bunch of shovels and come back up here one day real soon. And we're all gonna dig. And we're gonna dig and dig til we find that buried gold."

"Whoa!" says the Atom.

"Who's with me?" asked Billy.

"You mean….later today?"

"No. Not today," says the Brain. "We'll need more time, so we can plan. I wanna talk to Mr. Moldyman to learn where he read those legends about the pirates and their treasure."

Billy usually came up with the best plans. "Either way, we gotta do it before the next full moon. 'Cause that's when those ghosts will be coming back. Meanwhile, nobody says a word. Nobody else can know about the treasure."

We took another look at the footprints and spadework in the mud, at the huge char on the turret. The place gave me the creeps. Ping Pong finally put it best. "Let's just get outa here."

*****

The next day, Monday, we walked into Mr. Moldyman's classroom a few minutes early. Billy the Brain whispered to me and Cal, "Watch this. Watch me trick the old geezer." He walked up to Mr. Moldyman and the Brain says, "Hi, Mr. Moldyman. I was thinking…"

Mr. Moldyman looked up. "Yes, Billy?"

"I been thinking a lot about those pirate legends you told us about. I'd like to do some more reading about that, you know?"

"Billy, that's great! Sounds like I've got you interested in something!"

Billy played it cool. "You can say that again," Billy nodded. "Those legends. About our cove. Where can I read more?"

Mr. Moldyman looked at Billy with a big smile. "Give me a day or two. I'll be happy to make you a list." Billy returned to his seat and gave me and Cal the wink.

*****

The following day in history class Mr. Moldyman was speaking about Father Junipero Serra and his string of missions up and down the California coast. "What's a mission?" asked Ping Pong, not bothering to raise his hand from the back of the classroom.

"A mission is a church," answered Billy, looking up. "Dude. Didn't you read the homework? The guy built a bunch of churches." Billy shook his head and went back to his doodling. I peered across at Billy's paper. He tipped it up to give me a peek, and flashed his crafty smile. Whoa. Billy was drawing a *map.* In particular, it was a map of the bluffs at the top of the cliffs. He'd marked a circle where the lighthouse stood and added trees and the pathway and the fire-ring and some boulders. I motioned to Cal and we all watched as Billy the Brain lined out his treasure map.

Mr. Moldyman prattled on about California missions. My mind drifted back to the incredible storm last Saturday night and of course the flashes of lightning and the shifty figures we'd seen up on the cliffs. Mr. Moldyman talked about the swallows of Capistrano, how the flock returns to the mission on the same day each and every year. "Smart birds," says Cal. "Smarter than a stupid seagull."

That's when I heard the first tapping sound. It came from just outside the classroom. I thought nothing of it until the tap repeated itself and repeated again, from the hallway outside the room. It slowly grew louder, the taps were getting closer. Mr. Moldyman twitched and we saw his head flick slightly towards the door, towards this tapping sound. He continued to speak but the tapping grew brisk and was impossible to ignore. *Closer.* Then I realized what I was hearing. *Footsteps.*

Strange footsteps on the old wooden floor. Irregular. A guy with a limp?

Cal looked at me and Johnny. We looked at Billy who set down his pencil on his treasure map. We continued to hear a slow *clop clop. A plunk plunk.* Then the footsteps halted, just outside the classroom door. Mr. Moldyman had stopped talking.

All eyes in the classroom stared at the door. Slowly, the knob turned with its old rusty squeak and the door swung open. The footsteps began again. Ping Pong gasped. A figure stood in the doorway. A person from another era. He was from long long ago.

The man was tall with long filthy gray hair, tied in a ponytail behind him. He wore a long dark blue overcoat with brass buttons and a heavy collar. He was a heavy guy, pretty old. Grizzled. He had a black scarf round his neck and rough skin like a reddish pickle. He was tall and quite wide and none of us will ever forget his awful face and the crooked teeth and the weathered sneer. We could *smell* him clear in the back of the room.

Mr. Moldyman was fright-struck. Stunned, he backed away from the door, moving behind his desk, stumbling over his chair, bracing himself to the bookshelf with a noticeable gasp.

Clomp clomp. Plunk plunk. This brute walked to the center of the room, steps echoing off the wooden floor. That's when I noticed his leather boots. They were up around his trousers, almost knee-high, with brass buckles and curled leather straps. Old boots. The toes of one boot were torn and patched over with a hunk of leather, and nails stuck out holding it firm. And this man....this *pirate*....had something else. We all saw it. His disgusting boots were covered in mud.

He centered himself in the classroom just as one kid ran out the door. "Ay, ya coward!" the pirate screams, shaking his fist. Then he angled slightly so as to face our little group in the back corner. He lifted his cane and pointed it in our direction. The cane was shaking. He looked directly at us boys and I could see his wrinkled, shriveled eyes, and a line of spit moving down his chin.

I remember thinking, How did this guy know it was us? He opened his lips and inhaled air and spoke ever so slowly: "It's my treasure. It's my gold. You boys, *Leave it the hell alone.*"

Mr. Moldyman fell to his knees in the corner of the room. Ping Pong sat like stone, mouth stuck wide open. I had bumps on my skin and there wasn't a sound in the room. Then the old pirate turned, spat on the floor, *cursed*, and slowly clomped out of the room, leaving his stink and splots of mud. The door shut with a slam.

Every Hallboy in class moved *not an inch*. Mr. Moldyman sat on the floor, his face as pale as could be. We heard the gait of those steps – those boots – recede down the hallway, growing fainter. Me and Cal and Johnny…I could hear us breathing, panting as if we'd just run a mile.

"Wait a second!" exclaims Billy the Brain, finally breaking the silence. "What the heck? Ain't no way! Come on guys! Let's get him!" Billy leapt from his desk and ran for the door. Cal and I followed, with Johnny and the others close behind. "Let's get that joker!"

We tore across the classroom after the pirate, racing out the door. Looking down the hallway I knew we had him, with the boot marks and little clods of mud leading off. "HA!" yells Billy.

With fearless Billy leading the charge we dashed after him. He had no more than a 15 second head start on us. And the mud. Johnny the Atom took off and flew ahead. Wow, I remember thinking, we didn't call him the Atom for nothing. The mud trail led around the first corner to the staircase and there was no other way he could've gone. Down the stairs we dashed. From the bottom of the stairs the mud turned to the left, leading directly into the Parlor. I was just steps behind Johnny the Atom. We landed off the stairs and sped into the Parlor, mud marks still beneath our feet.

"Where is he!" shouts Johnny. "Where'd he go?"

A few Hallboys sat about on the various couches and loungers in the Parlor, reading or studying. There was no pirate to be seen. The muddy footprints led directly to the center of the Parlor, to the very middle of the old purple rug. There, they ended. Directly in front of the fireplace.

"The old pirate! He came right through here. Don't you smell that? Where'd he go?"

The Hallboys looked up at our anguished faces. "What the heck you talking about, Brain?"

"The big old man….the pirate! Where….?" Johnny and Cal knelt at the fireplace, craning their necks, looking up the chimney. A chimney escape? Impossible, we all thought.

The Hallboys looked at us with astonishment. Cal and Johnny dashed off, the other way, looking everywhere.

"This mud," shouts Billy. "The guy who tracked in all this mud? He was huge! He must've walked right past you guys!"

"Who?"

"The pirate!"

"Sure Chip. A pirate. You dudes are bonkers. You telling me a pirate came right through the Parlor and none of us saw him?"

"Look at the mud! He had mud all over his boots!" They looked down. Each Hallboy took notice of the boot marks across the floor, right to the middle of the purple rug, right in front of the fireplace, where they petered out.

"Looks like somebody forgot to do their Monday chores," says a Hallboy.

"I swear it was clean just a few minutes ago."

"Damn right it was clean. Wasn't no mud when I came in." We stood in the Parlor, looking at the mud, looking at each other. Billy the Brain scratched his head, flummoxed.

"Where's Ping Pong?"

"He's not here," says Billy. "Dang. He must've chickened out."

Cal and Johnny came running back in. "He's gone," they said. "We looked everywhere. Dude is gone!"

"What are you guys talking about?" asks a kid. "A pirate? Like, sure. You're nutzo."

"No!" says Cal. "Listen. Saturday night, the mud from the cliff tops..."

Billy the Brain quickly grabbed him by the elbow and says, "Cal! Shush it!"

"Huh?"

"Don't say a word," Billy says. "Wasn't *nothing!* It's a secret. None of us saw nothing."

$$* * * * *$$

Mr. Moldyman sat in Sniffy's Seaside Tavern across the table from a heavyset meat cutter named Deacon O'Dell who already smelled moderately of liquor. "Well, that was fun," said Deacon. "I bet we had more fun than those kids did. Except when that lightning bolt hit the damn turret. Crap. That almost killed us!"

"You put on a pretty good show as a pirate," Mr. Moldyman said. "Did you see the faces on those kids? They were *stunned.*"

"I make a damn good pirate, don't I?"

"An ugly old pirate," added Sniffy, the bartender.

"Teacher, you owe me a drink or two, no?"

"Yeah, yeah. Help yourself."

"How'd you like my costume? Not bad, huh?"

"Terrific! Where'd you get those old rags?"

"Down the street. The thrift stores. That's No Palms these days. One big second-hand shop."

"But tell me one thing," Mr. Moldyman asked the butcher. "When you left the classroom, and ran down the stairs. You left the trail of mud behind, all through the hall, right into the Parlor. Right up to the fireplace. Then it disappeared. Those kids were hot on your trail, right behind you. How'd you get away?"

"Easy!" Deacon says. "Can't you figure it out? I went into the Parlor *before* I stomped into your classroom. I smeared mud on my boots. I walked into the Parlor, across the rug, up to the fireplace. I left the trail *before* I came to your class. Then I took my boots off and backed out of the Parlor in my socks."

"No Hallboys saw you do it?"

"There were three or four laying around in there. I gave 'em each a couple bucks and told 'em to keep their yaps shut, if they knew what's good for 'em. Good upstanding Hallboys, can always keep a promise."

Mr. Moldyman nodded. "So after I stomped out of your classroom," the old butcher went on, "I ran down the damn stairs as fast as I could go. I knew they'd be right on my tail. I got to the bottom of the stairs, yanked off my boots like a maniac, and ran to the right, out the back door. The kids followed the trail of mud and ran to the left. Into the Parlor. I got away. Fooled 'em all."

Deacon O'Dell took a drink. "Fooled 'em all, except for one little Chinese kid. Brave little stinker. I don't think he was fooled one bit. I had a head start, but he chased me all the way across the great lawn. I beat him to the front gate but he kept coming. I went around the corner and dove into some old ladies' front yard, behind her damn gardenias. Right into her flower bed. Hid there like a thief until the little Chinaman went away. He was persistent."

The laughs went around the little tavern for a few minutes as the men ruminated and had a good chuckle. Everyone agreed that Mr. Moldyman had put together a good scheme. Then Deacon leaned into the table, close to Mr. Moldyman, and whispered, "You know why the lightning hit the turret, dontcha?"

Mr. Moldyman startled ever so slightly. "You mean, you've been thinking about that too?"

Deacon nodded. "Damn right I been thinking about it."

Mr. Moldyman looked back at Deacon, wary.

"There's a lot of metal underneath that turret, ain't there, teacher?"

"Yes, Deacon, that would be my guess."

"I'm right, ain't I," says Deacon O'Dell. "The treasure is still down there."

Mr. Moldyman sighed.

Deacon looked back at him. "So, tell me. You know those stinking kids. You think those curious little Hallboys would ever put two and two together?"

*****

Scottsdale, AZ

June, 2013

Copyright © Michael Daswick

FRONT PORCH

A t Boys Hall in No Palms, California, the best way to scrape seagull poop off the main gates is to use a putty knife and gasoline. As small boys we learned that ocean salt makes seagull poop especially sticking and corrosive. Why was I scraping seagull poop off the heavy iron gates that Monday at the orphanage? Punishment. Just another punishment assigned by the Head of the Hall for my misconduct.

"That's unbecoming of being a Hallboy. Scrape off the dried poop," the Head of the Hall said to me. "And don't chip the paint. Some of that poop has been there for years. Spray it with the gasoline first and let it soak through the poop." I looked at the white crust on the black iron bars of the gates. It looked like eggshell. *This is gonna take hours,* I thought to myself. "And when you're finished, sweep up your mess. I don't wanna see any crap on the sidewalk or the driveway. You got it?"

"You want me to do the whole entire gate? Today?"

"Yep. Both sides. Every damn inch. Bottom to top. Get a ladder if you have to." The Head of the Hall was a tired old man and we suspected that he drank a little bit when he was not messing with us Hallboys. He gave me a final look of disgust and trudged away, heading back up the long curving driveway to the main building.

My poop removal punishment was, I suppose, somewhat deserved. This particular episode began three days before on the Friday night as me and my pals Cal and Billy the Brain and a few other Hallboys were shooting pool in the dingy billiard and game room of the Hall. Billy, who fashioned himself as a surfer, was telling us how some old lady

had practically run him over with her car that very afternoon as he carried his surfboard across the Pacific Ocean Parkway. The P.O.P. is the
main drag through No Palms. It parallels the beach until it reaches the
pier and is lined with cruddy shops and businesses like the burger joint
and Sniffy's Tavern.

"Damn lady almost ran me over!" says Billy the Brain. "I was right
in the middle of the P.O.P. when this old bat almost flattened me. I
barely got out of the way! The old crow nearly clipped my surfboard. I
swear to God, she sped up when she saw me."

Billy the Brain was not prone to exaggeration "Was she from the
stinnkin' Women's Club?" our pal Cal asked.

"Oh, I'm sure she was. The witch. She didn't even steer around me!
In fact she veered over and tried to hit my board. I had to *hustle* to get
outa the way."

"That sorry old hag," Cal says.

Billy had some swear words for her, then said, "Maybe she'd been
drinkin' booze."

"Why do they hate us so much?" I asked.

"Who the hell knows," says Cal. "But they always have. Every old
bag at the No Palms Women's Club hates Hallboys."

"You shoulda seen her face as she zoomed by," says Billy. "She had
such a *sneer*. She looked at me like I was just some spit on the ground."

"They're all so lame over there," says Cal. "I mean, why be so bitter?
They got that great clubhouse. It's the best place in all of No Palms.
Right on the P.O.P. Hell, I wish we had a house like that."

"I'd like to take a leak on their Goddamn picket fence," says Billy.
"Or leave a dumper on their pretty little walkway."

Cal was aiming for the 8-ball. "I got a better idea," Cal says, his cue-
stick poised. "What about this: you know the rocking chairs that are

lined up on their front porch? What if we nail the rocking chair runners to the floorboards? Nail 'em straight into the floor!" Cal's eyes
were lit up. He focused hard on the 8 ball. He slammed it home. "What
do ya say? Ya wanna do it? Is it a plan?"

*****

So the plot was hatched. Cal worked it all out within minutes.
"Brain," he says. "Your job is to swipe a bunch of nails from the woodshop. Get long ones, at least two inches. Chip, you find a hammer. Get
a good heavy one. We'll go tomorrow night. Saturday night. Late. We'll
sneak outa here after the midnight bed-check."

"What about *you*, asks Billy the Brain. "Ain't you gonna do anything?"

"Don't worry, you moron. I'm gonna be doing the hammering."

*****

The next day, by noon on Saturday, Billy had a handful of nails
from the shop while I'd temporarily lifted a claw hammer from the jan-
itorial closet. Cal told us to wear dark shirts and we met in the second
floor bathroom at 12:30 AM.

"Are we gonna wear our caps?" I asked. Anytime a Hallboy stepped
off property, we were obliged to wear our purple caps.

"Yes," says Billy, with confidence. "I don't wanna be mistaken for a
local city kid!"

"You dudes ready?" Cal asked. "Let's go fix those chairs!" The
ground floor guard would still be awake so we shimmied out the bathroom window and dropped down the side of the building clinging to
the old brick outcroppings which were supposed to be ornamental.

Any Hallboy with a grain of agility had learned to scale these brick hand and footholds by the time they were six. The best climbers, of course, lived on the fourth or top floor. In any case, that Saturday night we dropped to the ground and crouched down. We could hear the waves breaking on the shore two blocks away.

Cal pointed across the great lawn to the main gates. It was a good night for mischief. Fog had rolled in from the ocean. I could barely see to the end of the driveway. Cal held up five fingers: he pulled in his thumb -- four; then he showed only three; two; one, Go! We dashed across the lawn, sprinting for the gates. It would creak like crazy if we opened it so we vaulted over the iron fence alongside. Once over and outside we lay flat on the sidewalk, breathing hard, looking back to the Hall through the fog. There wasn't a sound nor movement which might indicate we'd been spotted. Nor were there any cars in the street. Cal says, "Let's go," and we trotted down the Pacific Ocean Parkway through the fog towards the heart of No Palms and the Women's Club front porch, about ten blocks away.

Saturday night or not, the center of No Palms near the Women's Club was deserted and typically dismal. The neon glow of the big red nose sign above Sniffy's Tavern looked fuzzy through the fog. Town was dark and creepy. We sallied up to the white picket fence of the Women's Club and squatted low.

The No Palms Women's Clubhouse was an enormous old California craftsman cottage that was deeded to the Club years before. It was by far the finest looking building in town, maintained in pristine condition, in marked contrast to most of the shops and homes in No Palms which were in various states of dilapidation. At the women's clubhouse, the effects of fog, beachy salt air, age, and other weather were continually countered by regular maintenance and continual upkeep, right up to the fresh and famously pink paint on the front door. Behind the picket fence was a terrific garden with flower beds with plants and shrubs of all kinds. Exotics were a Club specialty. A sweeping raised porch wrapped three sides of the building. It's wooden floor and railings were shiny white.

There were rocking chairs on this nice front porch. Six of them, facing the P.O.P. Three on each side of the central front door.

The building was dark this time of night. Billy looked at me and I could tell this monkey business was making him nervous. Nonetheless we hopped the fence and scooted up onto the porch and ducked behind the railings. Cal pointed to the pink front door and says, "See that? They stole the idea from the Hall." The official color of Boys Hall was, of course, purple, and the Hall had had a purple front door for over 60 years, long before the Women's Club even came into existence.

"Gimme some nails," Cal whispers to Billy the Brain. "Chip, where's the hammer?" Cal scootched to the first rocking chair. It was a nice traditional wooden rocker with turned legs and spindles and a rich finish. The long runners curved elegantly. Cal gave it a little shove and it rocked slowly and smoothly, back and forth.

"Hurry it up," says Billy. "What if they have *cameras?*"

"These broads ain't got no cameras," Cal says. "The joint's deserted. The old bats have gone home. Stop being so nervous." Cal took a nail and positioned it over one of the runners. "Chip, hold the chair steady." I gripped the chair firmly with both hands. "Watch this," says Cal. He tapped the nail tentatively. The noise sounded horrific, reverberating off the porch and the side of the house. Cal stopped and looked up. We held our breath and looked across the street, up and down the P.O.P.

"Quiet!" says Billy.

"Shut up, Brain!"

I thought I heard an echo from the other side of the street. But nothing stirred but the fog and Cal let out a deep breath, looked at me, and resumed. He tapped the top of the nail. Tap tap tap. *Bap bap bap.* The entire floor of the porch seemed to shake but the nail started to go into the wood. "See how I put it in at an *angle*? That's to hold 'em better."

"You're a genius," says Billy the Brain.

BAM! BAM! BAM! The first nail went through the runner and at least an inch into the floorboards. "This is a piece of cake," says Cal. "Gimme another nail." Cal hammered the next one into the same runner, just a few inched further along, while I held the chair steady. He took a third one and said, "These bitchey bats are gonna have the surprise of their lives. Ain't no way these chairs are ever gonna rock."

All six chairs were nailed down within minutes. For the last three, Cal's impatience got the better of him and he paid no attention to the racket. He merely pounded nail after nail for all he was worth. Then he says, "What do the Goddamn seagulls say? Let's get the flock outa here!" Billy the Brain was already over the picket fence. We ran fast as snot down the P.O.P. before we had to stop. It is really hard to run when you are buckled over laughing.

*****

Before Sunday morning chapel and breakfast every Hallboy on the second floor knew what we'd done. They proclaimed Cal a brilliant hero and he relished in the attention and admiration. "Wouldn't you just love to see the stupid looks on their stupid faces when they sit down on their big butts and try to rock?" Cal asked. "I mean, how funny is that gonna be?" We laughed and all our imaginations worked through images of fuzzy-haired old biddies stuck still as they tried to lean back and tip.

"Guys," says Cal. "We just gotta go down there and watch. It's Sunday morning. The old broads....they'll be having their Sunday social today. They'll all be there. We gotta go. We gotta go watch the show!"

"You're nuts," says Billy. "Return to the scene of the crime? No way."

"Brain," says Cal. "How the hell would they possibly know it was us? I mean, we got outa there *Scott free.* We could go and stand in the middle of the front yard and laugh our asses off and they couldn't prove a damn thing. They couldn't prove it was us in a million years."

"Maybe not," says Billy, "but I ain't going back."

"How 'bout you, Chip. Wanna go with me? It's Sunday. We can get a Hall pass."

"Sure. I'll go. They can't prove crap. I'll go with you."

*****

Cal and I requested and received a three-hour Hall pass and we punched out at 9:30 am. We wore our purple caps. It was still foggy as we crossed the lawn and headed down the sidewalk of the P.O.P., giddy as we hurried along. When we neared downtown and the Women's Club I asked, "So... what are we gonna do?"

"Heck," says Cal with confidence. "We ain't gotta do nothing. We can just stand on the other side of the street and chase seagulls and watch. Ain't no law against that. Just don't crack up laughing when you see some old bat try to swing her chair. Har har!"

So Cal and I stood on the sidewalk across the street from the Women's Club, bothering birds and pretending to chat. One by one, old ladies arrived at their club, opening and shutting the small gate in the picket fence, walking up the porch steps, past the chairs, going inside the pink doors. "They'll come out sooner or later," says Cal. "Just wait and see."

"We only have a three hour pass. Hope we don't wait too long."

More women showed up. There were some passersby as well. In No Palms, you know everybody. "See that guy walking there?" I said to Cal. "With the big nose? That's Sniffy." A couple old men walked by with fishing poles, heading for the pier.

Then a small boy came along. "Hi Sherwin," we said. "Whazzup?"

Sherwin was about four years old. He wasn't a Hallboy but he came to the Hall from time to time to play with some of his pals. Everybody in No Palms knew Sherwin. He was a bouncy kid. We usually saw him on the pier and along the boardwalk where he'd try to mooch nickels and dimes so he could buy candy. That Sunday morning Sherwin was waving a five dollar bill.

"Where the heck you going with all that money?" Cal asks. "All by yourself."

"Going to the Little Store for my mama. Gonna buy some donuts."

"You better stop dawdling. Or I'm gonna steal your money."

"No you won't," says Sherwin happily, waving the bill as he skipped along. "It's from my mama. She gave it to me."

"You get along," says Cal firmly. "Go get your donuts and hurry home before you get robbed. There's mean people around here."

"No there aren't," chirps Sherwin, and he skipped merrily down the street.

Cal and I remained stationed on the P.O.P., loitering shamelessly, waiting for the little old ladies to finish their Sunday brunch and come out to their porch. Around 11:00 o'clock the pink door opened and two ladies drifted outside, holding tea cups. "See that?" says Cal. "They ain't gonna rock in no rocking chairs as long as they're sipping Goddamn tea and coffee."

Then things started to happen faster. Sherwin returned down the sidewalk from the Little Store swinging a box of donuts. A handful of ladies were spilling onto the porch. "Gramma! Gramma!" shouts Sherwin.

"Oh Shewwie baby! Hello Hello!" A little old lady on the porch waved her skinny little arm frantically. "Shewwie baby! Good morning!"

"Hallo Gramma." And Sherwin crossed the P.O.P. with his donuts and trotted through the gate and up the walkway onto the porch where he hugged his grandmother. All the other biddies closed around adorable little Sherwin. They cooed and gushed like happy seagulls as little Sherwin skipped about the porch from woman to woman. Moments later Sherwin couldn't resist: he dropped his donuts and sat down in one of the rocking chairs.

"Oh crap," mutters Cal.

Sherwin tipped back in the chair. Naturally, nothing happened. He leaned further back, but the chair remained perfectly still. Then, holding the armrests, Sherwin jerked forward. The chair didn't move an inch. Several ladies, perplexed, closed around. Sherwin continued to lean and jerk, forwards and backwards, back and forth. Cal's nailing job held superbly. One lady reached out for another one of the rockers. She pushed it but it didn't budge. The women on the porch began to buzz they looked at the other chairs. One bat bent down and examined the runners. She quickly removed her eyeglasses and stepped back as if she'd found a snake.

"Betty! Oh Betty! Come see this!"

Sherwin kept lunging. He threw back his head back and put the full force of his four year-old weight into the back of the chair. The women were gabbing and yakking as they took turns trying to move the rock-ers. Sherwin lurched up and down, growing ever frantic in his childish manner. He slammed backwards, he drove forward. Cal was giggling.

Then we heard a cold crisp *snap* from the front porch. Cal's angled nails did their job. However, the spindles of Sherwin's chair couldn't withstand his jerking. As he rammed forward the spindles suddenly snapped, catapulting Sherwin right through the porch railing. Sherwin flew ass over tea-kettle down into the flower beds. The women screamed. Sherwin landed face-first in some sort of hackleberry plant and burst into a piercing cry. "Wah! Waah! Waaah!" Initially, both Cal and I burst out laughing. Then we were horrorstruck.

Betty Battle, Chairwoman of the Club and well-known town grump, clamored down the steps and ran to the shrieking Sherwin, stumbling through the flowers, followed by the grandma. Then a wom-an on the porch raised her arm and pointed directly at me and Cal. "Betty, look. *Hallboys!*"

So what, I thought. We're just two kids out for a Sunday stroll on a Hall pass. You women can't do nothing to us.....

But Cal bolted. He says, "Holy crap!" and was off like a shot, sprint-ing down the P.O.P.

"Wait!" But he was long gone. So I raced after him. And comically, the pack of old bats came scurrying after me.

Cal ran past Sniffy's and the Little Store and over the boardwalk where he turned onto the pier. I chased him and the gaggle of biddies chased me. Cal and I ran through the fog all the way to the end of the pier. Had the women seen us? Oh yes they had. The angry mob had us cornered on the end of the pier.

"We're caught!"

Betty Battle was in front of the angry rabble of old bags. "Ha! Trapped like rats! You no gooders!"

The deck of the No Palms pier stands 30 or 40 feet above the ocean water. And the water is cold and deep.

"We can't just stand here," says Cal. "We gotta jump for it."

"Huh?"

"Jump!"

Cal was the best swimmer at the Hall. Far better than me. Without a flinch of hesitation he leapt the rail and plunged into the deep green sea far below. "Cal!" He took eight or nine fast strong strokes *straight out* away from the end of the pier before he disappeared into the fog. To this day, I never knew if he turned north or south before making it back to shore but he turned up a minute before his three hour Hall pass expired. In any event, Cal denied everything and was never caught. And Hallboy loyalty being what it is, I held my tongue and never ratted on him nor Billy either.

Betty Battle and her throng grabbed me and marched me directly to the Head of the Hall. I suffered his chastise and castigation and all the shame of holding a stinky rag, a jar filled with gasoline and a putty knife. Salty seagull poop locks on like crazy but when I was finished the front gates of Boys Hall hadn't been that clean in 15 years.

*****

December, 2012
Scottsdale, Arizona

THE BOYS HALL FISHING DERBY

The annual Boys Hall Fishing Derby was the event of the summer in No Palms. In the old days when the fishing from the pier was still pretty good, each Hallboy of every age would rather have the Fishing Derby than Christmas.

Boys Hall orphanage took over the town. And in a small little town on the coast like No Palms, our Derby was a perfect fit. To Hallboys, the Derby was far more than three days off property, and more than being on the town pier from sunrise Friday morning until sunset Sunday. Yes, we had big fun spreading sleeping bags on the old planks and feeling the sway of the old pier, moving with the summer swells; and the three-day barbeque fest on the Boardwalk with unlimited burgers, hot dogs, snacks, sodas and ice cream was a splurgerama. Never mind the non-stop fun and games, or the carnival show. Year-long double-dessert privileges to the winner? All this was secondary.

Hallboys loved the *buildup*. The competition. The Fishing Derby gave us all the opportunity to channel an unlimited helping of creativity into something that was very dear to us all. For months before, the Hall was alive with heckling, ribbing, pestering, bets, challenges, and (usually) good natured taunting. It was the most fun we were going to have all year.

Finally, the honor of holding the Grand Fishing Champion title was simply unsurpassed. The winning Hallboy would be *embraced* by one and all for the next 364 days. I cannot understate the prestige which accompanied this award. There was only one winner at the Derby. The Grand Champion. Weren't no secondary prizes, no runner-ups, no consolations. Accordingly, the cache that attached to this title, the acclaim and even *awe* from all other Hallboys and teachers was unrivaled. To have your name inscribed on the Grand Pacific Fishing Trophy – by far the largest trophy in the trophy case at Boys Hall – was the greatest recognition a Hallboy could receive. An A in algebra? Hallboys gave not a thought. Head of the class? Small or even no potatoes. However, in the life of a Hallboy, to be a Grand Champion of the fishing derby, that was unparalleled.

*****

The little chapel at Boys Halls was built as an extension off the main building. The Parlor in the main building was our living room, so to speak, and the chapel's proximity to the Parlor was such that relative quiet was required in both areas. As churches or even chapels go, ours was very small. There was a simple altar at one end, with plastic flowers, a cross, and three dead doves wired to a little branch, stuffed with cotton balls. Five rows of pews were set on either side of the central aisle. Carpet. A seldom-used upright piano stood in one corner with a Jesus candle on top. Stained glass windows were *painted* on the side walls, with crappy curtains, illuminated by pin-lights.

Hallboys were not required to attend church services. But most of us went anyways. Me and Cal, Billy the Brain, Johnny the Atom, Ping Pong. Many others. The Hall did have one chapel requirement: at an early age, every Hallboy had to attend a chapel orientation. This was when we learned the chapel rules if you did visit the chapel. We were used to rules at the Hall, but there was a separate and special chapel protocol. I had my first orientation at six years old. It was during this orientation that I learned all about religion at Boys Hall.

*****

Cheating at Boys Hall was, of course, strictly forbidden. Honor was supposed to be the foremost quality in any Hallboy's character and the Hall's Honor System was a cherished and vaunted tradition which, they say, was emulated by many many other orphanages and even colleges around the country. Ours was a *self-governing* program. The Honor System was enforced on Hallboys, by Hallboys. Cheating in the class-room, stealing from another, lying, fibbing, breaking rules, there was a zero tolerance policy against any transgression, no matter how petty. Cheating or deception in any form was not only viewed as an affront to our instructors and a dishonor to the long and storied history of the Hall, but was considered a stinging smear towards each and every Hallboy, whether that individual was a party to the deceit or not.

I'm pleased to report that the Honor System in place at the Hall was abided to. In fact, it was an element of great pride to almost every one of us. We were *proud* not to copy, peek at another's paper, plagiarize, or fib. Hallboys who routinely stole, cheated or defied the Honor System were held in very poor favor among the rest of us. They were pushed away from common games, dining tables, outings, clubs and events. And there was no benefit at all in being an outcast at Boys Hall.

*****

The build up to the Fishing Derby always began months prior to the event itself. With the Derby always scheduled for the last weekend in August, Hallboys began preparations as early as March or April, but Derby fever gripped us all by August 1st. That's the date when the Hall's plentiful stock of fishing poles and tackle was made available to everybody. August 1st was when each and every Hallboy commenced his personal – and highly secretive – strategy for that year. We plotted our secret bait. We hammered, forged, and bent special hooks. Derby month was a great time of togetherness, as every Hallboy worked towards the same goal, but a time of individualism as well, as each kid concocted their own winning game plan.

You had to make your bait appealing to a fish. So, from the cafeteria, we took spices, oils, seasonings, trimmings and ingredients, and mixed them like alchemists to find the ideal *flavor* that would be especially aromatic. Most critically, these blends must hold up on a lure or on a bait, and *in sea water.*

What would be attractive to a fish that year? That was anybody's guess. Billy the Brain said, "To win, you gotta think like a fish."

"Then how come you ain't won yet?" asked Cal.

"You gotta trick the fish," says Johnny the Atom.

"You gotta outsmart the fish," I added.

"Maybe I'm wrong," says Billy, "but you can't just think like a fish. To win, you gotta think like the *biggest* fish."

How did a kid win the Derby? Simple. You caught the heaviest fish. One winner. From sunrise Friday until sunset Sunday. The single heaviest fish won. One fish, one champ. Young kids, old kids. Everybody had a chance, everybody had high hopes. And one kid who had hopes as high as anyone – every year -- was the kid we called Craig the Cripple.

*****

The Hallmate of ours whom we affectionately called Craig the Cripple took his nickname from the physical disabilities that made him special. These disabilities included hands which were tight and twisted sideways at the wrists. His fingers were gnarled and they didn't close well or work like ours. Craig was born with these special limitations and while he learned to live with them to a certain degree, he was also helped by special adaptations. These adaptations included some handy gloves in which Craig could insert a crayon, a pencil, or even a paint-brush. Thusly he could draw and write and hold stuff. Craig the Cripple had something of a bent head as well, so he was always stooped, or head-cocked.

Accordingly, Craig was not very good at sports like other kids. He was awkward and clumsy. However, Craig loved to fish. He adored fishing. Too bad he was no good at that either.

Craig could barely hang onto a fishing pole. He didn't have an adaptive glove or grip for that. Moreover, casting and reeling were considerable challenges. He could release the reel and drop a line straight down into the water but he wasn't able to cast out. Tying knots was virtually impossible and he always got stuck by hooks and tangled his lines. Every Hallboy in our class had the fond memory of watching Craig the Cripple struggle with a wriggling worm with his goofy fingers, trying to stick it on a hook. Many a worm died between Craig's stiffened fingers before it could be pierced and plopped into the water.

The Hall made no special accommodations for Craig, as far as the Derby was concerned. Perhaps the Hall was a bit remiss in this area. After all, as I remember, we had no other Hallboys with disabilities except for the single year when Dead Eye Danny – a wheelchair user -- was with us. In any case, the fishing rules were very clear: as soon as the sun came up on Friday, Derby morning, nobody was allowed to receive help from anybody else. Period. During the Derby, you did everything on your own.

Of course, we loved Craig and while most Hallboys played football and baseball, we appreciated his efforts on the sidelines, season after season, where he helped with equipment and stuff, always cheering for the rest of us, clapping with his funny hands.

*****

Billy the Brain took his nickname one morning when we were small Hallboys, sitting over breakfast in the cafeteria dining room. Most of us spread marmalade on our toast. Billy chose not to eat marmalade, which the Hall bought in plastic gallon containers. I never saw Billy eat any. One day Billy took the bowl of marmalade and stuck a spoon in it and says, "Dudes. Look. Marmalade is nothing more than orange jam. It's just orange jam with a fancy name. But fancy name or not, Marmalade is still just lousy sour orange jam."

We watched Billy stir the marmalade with his spoon.

"Golly, Billy, you're a genius," says Cal. "You know that? You're a total genius. With comments like that, you oughta be called Billy the Brain." That was the first time anybody ever referred to Billy as a brain. The nickname stuck.

Not long thereafter our group of Hallboys was sitting in the small chapel, awaiting our first orientation session. We were six years old. The Head of the Hall gave us instructions as to how we were expected to act while in chapel. "Behave respectfully. Behave reverently whenever you enter the chapel. Keep your shoes on your feet and keep your feet off the benches." We sat in a line in the front row pew. Me, Cal, Billy, Craig, Johnny, a few more kids. "You're all expected to sit still. Don't squirm, don't distract your fellow Hallboys. And there's no gum."

That might be a toughie for Johnny, I thought.

"Don't talk. But if you do speak, *whisper.*" Then he says, very grave-ly, "And always remember: *God is watching you.*"

When we heard this we looked at each other. As six year olds, that comment had enormous impact upon us. Cal gulped. Then, after a few moments, Billy the Brain looked up, lifting his head towards the ceil-ing. Billy's eyes went up.

The Head of the Hall noticed Billy. The Head repeated, "Yes. God is watching you."

"How can God see us?" asks Billy.

"God sees everything."

"He can see us through the roof?"

"How?"

"He's God."

"Yeah. But then, how can he see every kid in every church? At the same time. All around the world?"

"He can not only see every kid in every church. He can see every kid *everywhere.* Every person everywhere. God watches *all of us.* Eve-rywhere. Every second of the day."

Billy and I exchanged glances. "How can he do that?" asks Billy.

"Because. God has five billion eyes."

"Five *billion?* Dang."

"Yes. And one eye is assigned to watch every single person, every-where in the world. That eye of God never leaves you." We exchanged glances at this thought.

"That's a lot of eyes."

"Of course it is. But that's how God can watch each of us. All the time. There's no fooling God."

"Do all those eyes *blink?*"

"I imagine so."

"Are they *big* eyes?"

"What do you mean?"

"Well, he must have a huge head."

"Yes. God is huge. He has an eye for each of us. And whenever a new baby is born, God adds another eye. A new eye to watch over that new child. God is adding eyes all the time. God is watching you, and god is watching *over* you as well."

"Wow."

So, for all us young Hallboys, that simple chapel orientation session turned into something much more profound. It was our first insight into actual *religion.* The impact on us was enormous and we walked out of chapel that morning, each of us in a slight state of shock. The thought that God had an eye, assigned solely to watch and watch over me, stayed within me for months, for years. Even til today.

*****

A day later we sat around the Parlor in front of the great fireplace and Cal tried to steal Craig's M&Ms. "Watch it!" says Johnny the Atom, pointing upwards. "God is watching you."

Cal says, "How can God have so many eyes? Five billion?"

"He must have eyes like a giant dragon fly," says Billy. "Dragon flies have these super-cool eyes that can see in every direction."

Craig the Cripple says, "You really think God looks like a giant dragon fly?"

"No, stupid," says Billy. "I didn't say God looked like a dragon fly. I was only talking about his eyes."

"Then what's God look like?"

"Don't be stupid. God looks like God."

"That's not the point," says Cal. "The point is that God's watching all of us. All the time. Five billion eyes. So he can watch all five billion people on earth. It makes total sense."

We were humbled by such knowledge. And I dare say that this had great influence on us in terms of limiting the cheating, fibbing, and dishonesty. "God is personally watching each of us," I reported. "That scares the heck out of me, but it also makes me feel good too. Nothing is gonna slip past him."

Therefore, and I can report this to be a fact: given what the Head of the Hall told us about God's incredible ability to watch every person on earth all the time, cheating at the Hall was truly low. The Boys Hall Honor System and God's five billion eyes truly worked.

*****

I never won the Boys Hall Fishing Derby. I came close one year when I landed a 19 pound reef shark. My bait? It was top secret of course, but that year I used garden snails. Slimy nasty garden snails. They were the oiliest, stinkiest thing I could think of. Several kids caught larger fish that year. The Grand Champion caught a 28 pound yellowtail tuna – a stunning catch. The picture of him holding up this monster is in the Hall gallery today. Another kid caught a nice sheepshead, and there were two or three bottom-feeding cod that were all larger than my shark.

Every year, everybody caught fish. In those days our little cliff-bound cove attracted all kinds of sea life. Most kids caught little one or two pound kelp-clippers or mini-mackerel. These weren't exactly keepers but it made everyone feel like they had a fighting chance. But sad as it was, year after year, Craig the Cripple caught absolutely *noth-*

ing. In all my adolescent years, I know for a fact that Craig couldn't even catch a smelt from the cannery floor. He didn't land as much as a tangle of seaweed. Not a bite, not a nibble. Try as he might, hands twisted around the rod, fingers flailing at the reel, line snagged time and time again on the pilings of the pier, Craig was shut out.

"You're pathetic," said Billy, who was the first of us to learn that word. "If they awarded a prize for the most inept fisherman, you'd win every year."

*****

We grew older, aged up, always abiding by the Hall's Honor System. Older Hallboys schooled the younger ones on the benefits of honestly and truthfulness. We took great pride that the incidence of cheating at the Hall was very low. We passed along the gospel that God had over five billion eyes and that he was watching, and watching over, all of us.

*****

When we were in 9th grade, the announcement was made for the dates of the 1970 Derby weekend. The official fishing Judges and Rules Committee sat behind a great desk in the Parlor while Hallboys jammed in to listen. It was August 1st. The Derby was a month away. The Head of the Hall, our history teacher Mr. Moldyman, and Coach Butterbar sat tableside looking very serious and all important. The Grand Pacific Fishing Trophy stood gleaming in the center. The Head of the Hall gave the Silence sign and cleared his throat.

"The 43rd annual Boys Hall Fishing Derby will commence upon the first glimpse of the sun on Friday, August 29, and end upon the final flash of sunset on Sunday, August 31. As usual, the Hallboy who lands, by himself, the heaviest fish, will be declared the Grand Champion. His name will be engraved on the Grand Pacific Fishing Trophy." There was a big Hallboy roar. Whistles and clapping ensued until the Silence sign appeared again. "As usual, the scale in the gym locker room will be the official measure of weight. Also, as usual, there will be no classes held on the preceding Thursday, August 28th." Biggest cheer yet. "Fishing poles and tackle will be distributed from the commissary building beginning at 2 pm today. Hallboys, I hereby declare the 1970 Fishing Derby officially *OPEN!!*"

Every Hallboy whooped and shouted. The Parlor sprang to life. Kids tore off to the workshop, gardens, cafeteria, lawns, labs, and art room to gather supplies, fabricate lures, to scheme and scam. Each and every one of tinkered with highly clandestine concoctions; we hammered sinkers, strengthened leaders, we sharpened the barbs on our hooks. To attract fish, creative Hallboys fashioned lures out of everything imaginable…anything to catch the light and sparkle for a moment: flashlight bulbs; jackknives; forks and spoons removed from the cafeteria, coins, broken glass, a bent-up bottle-cap. Kids sanded and whittling wood into every shape.

Somebody saw Craig the Cripple gathering seagull feathers behind the laundry and the rumor spread that fish were wild about seagull plumage, especially if the bird was wounded. This gave many Hallboys still another reason to slingshot a seagull. "Seagull feathers?" asked Billy the Brain. "The Cripple thought of that?" There was no end to the size and shape of the lures that we worked up. Broken marbles for eyes; nails for legs. We caught bugs. We dug for worms. Saved cheese. Shaved turnips. Carved potatoes. Skinned carrots. Clipped candles into shapes like tadpoles and newts. We scavenged sand-crabs, hacked barnacles off the pier pilings. Johnny even chewed steak, spit it out and squeezed it into minnows. Cal speared a red butterfly. A pop-top – twisted a certain way -- would make a lure spin; wire from a Hall lamp; matches; a tuft of insulation, flower petals carefully cut and shaped into fins and tails.

Anticipation for the 1970 Derby was sky high. Personally, I was as hopeful as any other Hallboy. I built 6 lures. My best one, or my favorite, upon which I based most of my hopes, was made from some leather from a smelly old baseball mitt soaked in cod liver oil, a piece of a rake handle, silver duct tape, aluminum foil, and raisins which I glued on for eyes. I hollowed out the piece of rake handle and smeared peanut butter inside. It had all kinds of good smells and jerked along as if wounded. It had plenty of magic. When the lure got wet, the peanut butter would slowly dissolve, soak through the tape, wafting aroma of peanut butter through the water, attracting an undersea monster. I tested the percolation factor many times in the bathroom. I found the exact pressure with which to wrap the tape: not too tight, not too loose. This allowed for a gradual release of eau de peanut butter and cod liver oil into No Palms cove. I shared this scheme, of course, with absolutely nobody.

Cal devised his own strategy. Cal loved to watch the tides and the weather. "Chip," he whispers one night. "Which side of the pier you are gonna set up on?"

"Neither. I'm fishin' from the very end."

Cal pursed his lips. "Listen, pal. Normally, everybody wants to be on the north side, 'cause it faces the cove. But this year, at the end of August, there'll likely be hurricanes way out in the Pacific. There'll probably be a big swell rolling in from the south. The bigger fish will chase the smaller fish who'll get pushed in on these swells. So you wanna be on the *south* side of the pier, and catch 'em when they come in."

"No," says I. "The little fish will be scared. They'll want the shelter of the cove. Big fish eat little fish, so the biggies will go into the cove too, to hunt. Ya gotta go to the north side. Facing the cove."

"You're nuts. You gotta face the swells. And fish in the evening. When all the little Hallboys get tired."

And so forth. That was the kind of conversation on everybody's lips in Boys Hall every August as the Derby grew closer. Strategies, schemes, theories, optimism and dreams – all in great abundance. The Grand Pacific Fishing Trophy stood on a pedestal in the main entry foyer. Past champions walked around property like celebrities.

One day in late August Cal, Billy and I walked into the woodshop to get glue and clamps. Craig the Cripple was leaning on a workbench. He had a wooden dowel in a vice and was trying to file ridges and lines into the dowel. The metal file was skinny and with his clumsy fingers, Craig had great difficulty gripping the tool. He could make two or three passes with the file before it fell from his fingers and clattered to the bench.

"Lemme help you," Cal says. "Gimme that file. I'll help you score those lines."

"I can do it," Craig shot back.

"Crip. You've been working on this same lure for days. Let us help you while we can. Look how choppy this is. Ain't no fish gonna want to eat this ugly thing."

"Yes they will."

"No way, Craig," Billy spoke up. "This is ugly. You'll scare every-thing away."

Well, that comment hurt Craig's feelings. He tossed the file to the floor, turned his back and says, "I'm doing the best I can. But I can't do it. Every year, it's always the same. I ain't never even gotten a lousy bite in the Derby. And I ain't gonna get one this year neither, let alone hook a fish. Let alone actually *win* the whole stupid thing. I hate the stupid Derby!"

"Craig," yells Billy the Brain. "Knock it off. Stop pouting, dammit."

"Well, it's true."

"It might be true but you don't have to be a baby about it. If you want help, we're all here to help. But dude! Nobody wants to help a baby. Stop the whining. If you want something down, ask for help. If you don't wanna ask for help, then get the hell outa the woodshop and go dig for worms or something."

Craig told Billy to get lost. He was too proud to ask for help, and too proud to give up. We saw him tinkering, and he shielded his creations from us whenever we tried to take a look.

*****

On the morning of the Boys Hall Fishing Derby, the No Palms pier was lined with Hallboys, all standing shoulder to shoulder around the railings from the shore break outwards. Naturally, all of us wore our required purple caps. Since overhead casting was not allowed on the No Palms pier, our fishing poles were poised, over the rails. It was dark, just after 5 am. The two red lights on the end of our pier blinked and we heard the swoosh of ocean water going past the pilings. Every Hallboy stared towards the east where a rosy sky crept higher. It was a clear summer morning. As soon as the leading edge of the sun burst over the hills the judges would toot the horn and every Hallboy would cast off.

I stood at the north corner of the end of the pier. The perfect spot. My peanut butter mega-special dangled a few feet over the dark Pacific. Cal was on the southern side watching the swells roll through the phosphorescence. Billy went counter to all the orthodox thinking. He was far down the pier, in towards shore, near the wave-break. It's too shallow in there, I thought. Too muddy. But Billy must know something that we don't know! Such was the angst of the Hallboy fishermen.

Johnny the Atom, I suspected, was using pickle juice. And Craig the Cripple stood in a cluster of kids, facing the cove. I recognized him a hundred yards away, trying to get his reel to cooperate with his hands. Kids checked the weight of their sinkers. Bobbers were fastened and secret baits were removed from tackle bags. A rash of predatory seagulls circled overhead.

All eyes to the east, a string of purple caps around the edge of the pier, the very first glint of the sun's disc sparked above the hills. The Hall foghorn blasted across the water and a chorus of shouts erupted and could be heard all along the Pacific Ocean Parkway. Immediately, hundreds of lures, bobbers, sinkers, hooks, and fishing contraptions splashed into the ocean. Kids cast off beneath the pilings, flipping their tackle as far out from the pier as possible. Immediately thereafter, the predictable shouts of anger and accusation: "Hey! You tangled me! You crossed my line! You casted sideways! Stop reeling! What the heck? No! Not there! Moron! I'm hooked!..." In the first frantic two minutes of the Derby, year after year, dozens of kids tangled together. Lines up, lines down. In and out. At the start it was exactly the same each year: still in the dark, boys huddled together with flashlights trying to detangle the messes that were inevitable in those close quarters.

In 1970 a second grader caught the first fish. A four pound sheepshead – a common fish that lingers around the pilings of many So Cal piers. The little lad screamed as his fish flopped about on the deck. "What was his bait?" "What'd he use?" "Seagull egg!" "No way!" We all strained to look at the sheepshead. Just a small one, I thought. Happy little kid. He wasn't gonna be shut out. But a four pounder? Ain't no winning fish.

The barbeques were flaming by 8 am and without a nibble on my peanut butter special I stopped for a morning cheeseburger and a soda and took a stroll around. Billy was concentrating on the action of his bait. Lift it up five feet, drop it down five feet. Up and down.

"Got any nibbles yet?"

"Crap no."

Cal had no luck either. "It's only 8:30. We got three days to go. But look at the swells. They're rolling in, just like I told you. And it's still early. High tide today is noon-thirty. You'll want your bait in the water exactly then."

Craig the Cripple felt for the most minimal vibration on his line. When the kid next to him jerked upwards, coiling Craig's line, Craig sulked. "I said *under*. You went *over*. Now we got a real mess." Craig's claw-like hands couldn't unravel the lines. The other kid wanted to cut free and start over. Craig knew if he did so, he'd lose his lure. Total disaster. And he could never be able to restring his tackle. He couldn't tie lines at all. Getting help from others – now that the Derby had started, was cheating. And Craig knew: one of God's five billion eyes was watching him.

*****

At the halfway point on Saturday the leading fish was a 26 pound albacore tuna that had somehow ventured into No Palms waters. This wasn't good news; that was a nice fish. It'd be awfully tough to beat. Billy the Brain looked at the huge fish: "You usually find albacore 50 or 60 miles off shore. In schools. Normally, they don't come in close. It's an aggressive fish. Hard to catch. The guy who caught this one is one lucky Hallboy."

The guy who caught the albacore was a smug senior who was due to age out of the Hall in just a few months. He refused to say what he used for bait, and while nobody could blame him for that, we didn't like his smug superior attitude. Cal and I stared down at his fish. "Beat that one," says the kid. "I double dog dare you."

Fish did not like peanut butter or baseball leather soaked in liver oil. My theory was all wet. I'd moved to my back up lures, and then to my back up back ups. Cal studied the August swell and we marveled as those rollers climbed and peaked into waves which blasted against the base of the cliffs in the No Palms cove. "The swells are too big," Cal says. "Fish get seasick too. When it gets rough like this they dive down deep. Drop your lines way way down. Get beneath the turbulence."

Billy had caught five fish. He had them lined up behind his tackle bag. Of course, his largest was two pounds. Johnny the Atom looked down and said, "Brain. What do you call those? Bait? Ha!!"

Craig the Cripple had a small pile of kelp to show for his efforts by the time he labored to crack open a can of pop at 8 pm Saturday night. Poor guy, I thought. Billy kicked the seaweed. "Cripple," he says. "Maybe you oughta just give up."

*****

Many Hallboys did just that. They gave up. And it was only Saturday night. With the senior kid parading his 26 pound albacore up and down the pier, laughing at the two and three pounders at the bottom of some buckets, discouragement was rampant. When that creepy kid sat on the victory stand itself as if he owned it, I could hear Johnny the

Atom swear under his breath. The hot August sun and two solid days of relative boredom sitting on the pier tested our mettle. Around 8 pm with the sun setting fast me and Cal and Billy wrapped it up for the night and we went back for another hotdog dinner. As we put on the fixins we saw Craig the Cripple fighting with a cork fishing float. "Whatcha got there, Crip?" asks Billy.

"Itsa big hunka cork."

"Whatcha doin with that big hunka cork?"

"Gonna see if this float can catch the breeze and the swell and drift out into the middle of the cove."

Billy looked at me and Cal. His eyebrows went up. "Crip? *You* thought of that?" Billy was quite sincere. "Genius."

"Go for it," I added. "Just hope this breeze keeps blowing in the morning."

"I ain't waiting til the morning," says Craig. "I'm still fishing now. I'll be night fishing."

"*Night fishing?*" asks Billy. "Crip! Don't do that. Go get a burger and hang out with us. You don't wanna be fishing at night."

"I'm gonna fish *all night* until I get a damn bite."

Night fishing, while certainly allowed during the Derby, was considered the height of desperation. With almost every single Hallboy rolling out his bedroll or sleeping bag on the deck, trays of s'mores and tubs of ice cream at the ready, the evening's tomfoolery and shenanigans were about to begin. This was considered prime time, one of the very few nights of the year when we were all off property. "Craig," says Cal. "Hang with us, dude. You don't wanna be watching no fishing line in the dead of night."

"I got a flashlight."

"That crappy thing? Even with a good flashlight you can't see nothing down there."

Billy added, "And Crip, the fish can't see nothing either. The water's too dark. And fish need to sleep too. They're sound asleep. Trust me."

"Craig, get a popsicle. You'll feel better. None of us have caught anything decent. Please don't night fish. Roll your bag by mine. We got room. You'll hook into something tomorrow."

"I'm gonna night fish," Craig said, determined. "All night long if I have to."

Billy shrugged. Billy looked at his burger and broke off a piece and offered it to Craig. "Here, dude. Eat this."

"Sure," says Craig. "I can try it as bait."

*****

At one in the morning every star in the universe was up above the No Palms pier. Every Hallboy could name the constellations and the smarter ones could point out the planets. Midnight stories had wound down and besides the occasional giggles and gassers, most kids were asleep. The *whump* of the waves blasted the cliffs. Billy says, "Come on. Let's check on the Crip."

We found Craig awake on the far northern corner of the pier. His flashlight batteries were dead. His line angled down into the darkness. His big fat float was somewhere on the black water. "The cheeseburger as fish bait didn't work too good," he says.

"I wanted you to eat it, Cripple. Not fish with it."

"I know. But I'll try anything these days."

"A nibble? Anything?"

"Nada. Nothin'." Craig was utterly forlorn, completely despondent. Billy said, "Hey Craig, you missed all the good stories. Reel that thing in, let's get some sleep. Want an ice cream? I know where they put 'em away."

"Do you think fish eat ice cream?"

"Dude. Come on, bag it. We'll all try again in the morning."

"I'm staying here."

*****

At 6:30 Sunday morning, the sun already up in the sky, we went to see Craig. He sat in the same exact spot. We looked down into the water. The line to his fancy cork float was snagged around the pier piling directly beneath him. The hunk of cork was knotted against the black barnacles. "It never even floated past the pilings," Craig says. "It was too dark to see, but it never got out into the cove. I wasted the whole night." Craig's forehead rested against the railing. "Rats."

*****

By 3 pm on Sunday afternoon only about 25 Hallboy fishermen remained. Cal left and was swimming near the old walled beach beneath the cannery. Johnny the Atom was behind the barbeque, flipping burgers. Me, Billy and Craig were still fishing. I leaned my pole against the rail and walked over to Billy's position. "How long you gonna hang?" I asked.

"I donno. Maybe another hour. I'm not sure I can make it til sunset. I think the fish are pretty damn confused by now. It happens every year."

A shriek of panic shot out from the other side of the pier. We spun to look. "Craig!"

Craig the Cripple was on tip toes, bent double, leaning way over the rail. His fishing pole was clutched in front and bent into a sharp arch, jerking erratically. The line was taught and angled away while the reel screamed, spinning wildly, line zipping out as fast as the reel could turn.

"Cripple!" yells Billy. "Hang on, dude!" We rushed over and I grabbed Craig by the back of his shorts so he wouldn't fall overboard. The reel zinged like mad as Craig clutched at the rod with the most improbable grip. He held it mostly with the palms of his hands, while his crooked fingers curved in, barely able to touch the rod. "Hang on to it, Buddy," yells Billy. "You can do it! Don't let go!"

"What it is?" Craig screams.

We stood in awe, watching fishing line tear away, the reel spinning like crazy. A crowd quickly pressed around, all the kids, judges, by-standers.

It's a monster!" yells Billy.

"It's sure as heck more than 26 pounds! Just hang on!" Whatever was on the end of Craig's line, it'd taken the bait, got real mad, and raced straight away from the pier at breakneck speed, heading out to sea.

"You gotta tighten down the drag!" Billy yelled. "You gotta screw down the drag!"

In all my childhood years fishing on the No Palms pier, in the Derby and otherwise, I can never remember anyone ever catching anything large enough to require a tighter drag. Nonetheless, Billy kept screaming, "Crip! Tighten the drag!"

"What's the drag?" Craig yells back, arms shaking. "What...what do I do?"

"Turn that dial on the right side." Billy leaned over the rail and pointed to the mechanism on the reel. "That thing right there. Turn it towards you."

All of us looked at Craig's hands, his palms pressing together, his fingers virtually useless. "I can't! I'll drop the pole!"

"Turn it, Cripple. Look! You're gonna run outa line!"

"I can't!"

"Turn it!"

"I can't! I can't!"

We all saw Craig's predicament. The way his hands were, it was impossible for him to hang on to the pole and turn the drag wheel. His fingers simply did not have that kind of agility. Meanwhile, the line had played out almost to the bare metal drum.

"Lemme do it," says Billy. "Here, dammit."

"No! I gotta do it myself!"

"I'll help you."

"You can't!"

"You'll lose the fish!"

"It's cheating!"

Technically, of course, Craig was correct. Everybody knew that Derby rules strictly prohibited assistance, help, or teamwork of any kind. We all knew it. But Billy the Brain did it anyways. The line was running out. Billy reached out, touched the reel, and turned the drag wheel half a turn towards Craig. "Nooooo!"

The reel ground to a halt. It groaned, there was a metallic sound, but it stopped turning. "See?" says Billy. "That was all you needed. Now just hang on and catch your breath." With the added tension the arch of the pole narrowed.

"No no no! I won't be able to…."

"Just hold on!"

"No!"

SNAP!

Craig's pole whipped straight. The broken fishing line feathered in the breeze. Every pair of eyes on the pier stared straight out to the empty ocean. Craig dropped his head onto his shaking arms. "Dammit. It's gone."

Craig the Cripple heaved back away from the rail, dropped his pole and collapsed on the deck of the pier. Billy looked at me, helpless. Craig began to cry. "Brain, you had to touch it. You had to! You made the line break!"

"Dude! You were gonna lose the fish! You had maybe 15 feet of line left! Your line was gone! Look at the reel. See? There's nothing left!"

"But you had to touch it! I told you not to. It was my fish!"

"Crip," I says. "You battled that giant toe to toe."

"Brain...what do you think it was?" asks some kid. "What did the Cripple hook into? Didja see what it was doin' to that reel?"

Billy looked from Craig to me to the kids to the endless ocean. "I dunno, guys. He must've had a brute. A monster. It was something huge."

*****

Well, Craig refused to speak to Billy. Billy pleaded for understanding but he finally slunked away like a broken boy. Craig pouted, but only for a few minutes. Then, oddly invigorated by his incredible strike, he hastened to grab another rod and get a new line right back in. He baited up a simple wad of cheddar on a hook with a two ounce sinker and at 5:45 pm, Craig was back in the water while the Hallboys moaned about The One that Got Away. Half the kids said, "Billy's an idiot," while the other half said, "At least Billy gave it a try. He had to try to save the fish."

*****

I was eating my 13th or 14th cheeseburger of the weekend at 6:45 Sunday evening. As was Derby tradition, every Hallboy returned to the pier to watch the sun set into the Pacific, into a spot just off the hazy outline of Catalina Island far away on the horizon. Several Hallboys fished right up until the final minutes. One of them was Craig the Cripple, who gazed off into the blue Pacific, seemingly in a daze, still pondering the lost possibilities of what might've been. Craig played those four or five frenzied minutes over and over in his mind. What took his lure? How big a fish was it? It was so powerful. What could he have done? Did Billy ruin his chances? The line would've run out, Billy was right about that. The reel was down to the last few turns. In any case, just another year without so much as a stinking sardine.

Craig checked the sun. It burned about 30 minutes over the horizon.

That's when Craig felt two sharp tugs on his line. Craig's palms tightened around the fishing rod. Tug Tug. There it was again. Sharp and distinct. Just a big swell going by? No way, Craig thought. That wasn't no wave. But it wasn't a nibble either. It was far too strong. Then he felt action again. Tug Tug. JERK! Whoa! A bite. A *big* bite! Something down there is going after my sharp cheddar cheese! And with that, Craig's pole fell hard against the railings, pulled straight downward by a forceful, almost violent motion.

"Hey…" stammers Craig. "Hey guys….I got….I got something again! Look at my pole!" Hallboys shot over to Craig's station. His rod was set heavily against the top of the rail. The tip curled straight down, pointing directly to the water below. His line taught, straight into the sea. With the excitement, nature caused Craig's hands to clench tighter, his fingers trying to dig into the cork handle.

"What is it, Crip? You got another?"

"The Cripple's got something! The Cripple's got a fish on!"

Craig held on for dear life. No line was streaming out. The drag was holding. It looked like Craig was in for a fight.

"Holy crap," says Johnny the Atom, looking at the pole quiver.

"Hang on, Craig," yells Cal. "Hang on!"

"You sure it ain't a snag?" asks some kid.

"Ain't no snag," says Craig. "I felt it tug. A big bite. Then it tugged again. Three times in all. It ain't no snag."

"Can you reel it up at all? Can you crank it?"

Craig tried. He adjusted his fingers slightly, but we could tell it was all he could do to merely hang onto the rod. "I can't do it. I'll drop it!"

"Try, Craig. Try!"

"Dammit!" Craig moved the base of the rod and planted it underneath his armpit. This gave him a little more control and leverage. He slid his hand down to the reel and hooked his fingers onto the handle. With great effort Craig managed to turn the reel one revolution. The line came up three inches.

"Way to go, Crip," someone yelled. "Again! Again!"

Craig set his hands once more. This small movement – against whatever type of beast was lurking below -- took enormous effort. "It's way down there," Cal says. "Craig. You gotta keep turning it."

"I'm trying, I'm trying!"

Johnny the Atom glanced at the sun, which was dropping fast, nearing the horizon. "Whatever you got there, Craig, you gotta have it on the pier by sunset," Johnny said. "I'd say that gives you six or seven minutes." Craig grimaced. He cranked again and gained another three inches of line. All of us pressing around were painfully aware of one thing: in the ten minutes he'd spent fighting his fish, Craig had only accomplished only two measly turns of the reel.

"Reel it, Crip!" yells a Hallboy. "Reel it! Reel it!"

"You can do it!"

"Fight it! Land it!"

Craig glanced to see the sun edging towards the horizon. His hands closed slightly and there was a bit of motion and we saw Craig catch a certain rhythm: he began to turn the reel. Once. Twice. 3, 4, 5. 10, 11, 12 times. "Yes!" we all yelled. Then Craig lost his grip and the pole bounced on the rail. "Dude! Hang on!"

"Craig…you had it. Reel it again."

Craig found his rhythm one more time. 5, 10, 15 turns. He was gaining on it! We looked down, into the sea, but all we saw was a straight line going vertical into the water. The sun touched the horizon. Cal yelled. Johnny screamed in Craig's ear: "Reel it!" I figured there were two or three minutes left in the Derby, tops. Craig fought and achieved 15, maybe 20 turns. Again, we looked down. And out of the murk, a strange, silver brown shape appeared a few feet beneath the surface.

"Color!" yells a kid. "Pull, Craig, pull!"

Ten more turns. The head of a large strange fish broke the surface. Ugly, wrinkled, what the heck did he catch? And the fish was not fighting back. It merely hung there on the end of the line.

"Halibut!" shouts a kid. "He's got a halibut!" We gaped. Sure enough, a wide, flat brown flounder-type fish, hung half out of the water.

"The sun! Look!" Only the top half was visible. The horizon sliced it in two.

"Craig…go!"

The distance from the ocean surface to the deck on the No Palms pier is about 35 feet. There was no possible way Craig could've reeled that fish all the way up in less than a minute. Cal looked at the sun. Then he looked at me. Johnny looked at Cal.

The three of us moved as one. Cal grabbed the middle of Craig's fishing rod. Johnny grabbed the reel. I took hold of the line itself. Together, the four of us began to pull that halibut up as fast as we possibly could.

"No!" shouts Craig. "NOOO!"

I gathered line, hand over hand. The fish broke clear of the water. It was indeed a halibut. It swung awkwardly back and forth. "Let's go guys," yells Cal. "Let's go!"

"Hey! The Crip's getting help!" somebody had the audacity to shout out. "They're helping the Crip!"

"Nice fish!" someone calls. "It's a fatty!"

"But it's no winner. It ain't no 26 pounder."

I kept looking down as I hauled up the fish. I'll report that it was not the largest halibut ever. It was about two and a half feet long. But as I collected line, as we heaved it upwards, all I could think was, *"Damn* is this thing *heavy."*

My hands bled from the line. We fought. The fish neared deck level. "Pull!" I hauled up one final time as Craig and Cal and Johnny lifted the pole. The halibut slammed onto the decking with an awkward *Tha-wump.* All eyes turned instinctively towards the setting sun.

There it was, just the top edge of the disc. There was a little flash, and the sun was gone. Craig's fish was on deck just in time.

All eyes whirled back to the halibut, which lay on its flat stomach, twisted eyes looking crazy to the right. It was about as long as a baseball bat. The crush of Hallboys gasped. Craig, me, Johnny and Cal panted. Then some kid says, "What the heck kinda halibut is *that?*"

"Cripple, what did you catch?"

"Holy smokes, Crip. Your fish is shaped like a *whale!*"

Sitting on the old splintered planks of the pier before us was indeed a nice but fairly unremarkable fish. The question was, what the devil was *inside* the halibut?

The judges closed around. On first glance it appeared that the fish had eaten a stack of dictionaries. There was some type of *rectangle* inside the fish. While the halibut was flat on its belly and sides and head, there was a grotesque block-like anomaly within. This block stood straight up, with the skin pulled tight all around. Like a shoe box.

The Head of the Hal and Judges Moldyman and Butterbar approached the fish cautiously. They leaned over in the twilight touching it gingerly, pressing along the edges of the cube within. The fish, by the way, looked pretty dead to me. "It's as hard as it can be," says Mr. Moldyman, inspecting all sides of it. Somebody handed them a flashlight. Carefully, they rolled the fish over.

"Something's inside," says the Head of the Hall. "But whatever it is, I have no idea how it got there. There's no cuts or scars. The skin is intact all the way around, top and bottom, everywhere. How would it eat...? Whatever is inside, it was way too big to fit through its mouth. Way too big."

"What could it be," asks Mr. Moldyman, utterly befuddled. "I know one thing, however," he says while Craig posed for a picture with the fish. "We gotta get this fish on the scale. Let's weigh this fish right now."

*****

August 31 had been another delightful summer afternoon at the No Palms Womens Club. A lovely Sunday afternoon, I suppose, until Club President Betty Battle left to go home. At 7 pm the day was winding down and Betty bid Bye Bye to the remaining ladies who sat about the front porch of the Club. She walked to her car, sat down and turned the key. Betty's car wouldn't start. There wasn't as much as a groan from the ignition. Betty knew nothing about automobile engines but she looked underneath the hood anyways. She immediately saw the problem. Her car battery was gone missing.

*****

"51 pounds, 8 ounces," Judge Butterbar announced.

"Yeah but what's inside it?"

"I have absolutely no idea."

"We know. Open its mouth and look inside." The judges looked at each other. "That's exactly what we will do. Where's that flashlight?"

On hands and knees, the judges used pencils and pliers to pry the halibut's mouth as wide open as possible. Mr. Moldyman leaned down, cheek against the planks, and shone the flashlight into the fish's mouth. We held our breath. He manipulated the pencils and the pliers to gain a better view. After a minute he raised up, removed his glasses, shook his head and says, "Craig Fairchild. That fish of yours…." he pointed, "has swallowed a car battery."

*****

"Cheater! Cheaters!"

The cry went up almost immediately.

"The Cripple is a cheater!"

"And they helped him land it. Cheaters!"

"And there's a car battery inside. Double cheaters!"

Craig looked aghast, his eyes fixed on his remarkable fish. Then he looked up, into the crowd. Standing on the fringe stood Billy the Brain. I saw that Billy's hair was soaking wet beneath his purple Hallboy cap. There was a small puddle of water around his shoes. That boy, thinks I, just went for a swim. Craig frowned and lowered his eyes back to the halibut.

*****

The Boys Hall Fishing Derby Judges and Rules Committee were convened between the two blinking red lights on the end of the No Palms pier. Their job was to declare a winner of the 1970 Derby. They were in deep conversation. The Hallboys kept a close eye on their deliberations while we mobbed Craig and ate cheeseburgers and ice cream sandwiches. The senior kid paced nervously back and forth, near to the judges, muttering "I caught my 26 pounder fair and square. Fair and Square. And there wasn't no car battery inside."

The kids were feeling Craig's halibut. They were looking for any opening whatsoever. "Gross! You can feel the corners. You can even feel the terminals through the skin! How'd it get in there?"

The judges gathered behind the table which held the Grand Pacific Fishing Trophy. "The winner, of the 1970 Boys Hall Fishing Derby is…with a halibut weighing in at 51 pounds and 8 ounces.....***Craig Fairchild!***"

The pier erupted. Hallboys waved their purple cps while poor loser senior kid skulked away, cussing and moaning, No fair, no fair. Cal, Billy, Johnny and I were the first to congratulate Craig, who made his way alongside the judges, behind the trophy table. The Head of the Hall and the other judges shook Craig's gnarled hand and patted him on the back. He stood behind the table with his famously half-cocked head, looking bewildered.

"Thank you so much," says Craig, after the crowd had quieted down. Then Craig began to cry. "But I can't be the winner. I didn't win. I didn't catch this thing. I....I cheated. You ain't supposed to cheat. But I cheated. I got help, and Billy cheated too." Craig, still wailing, neck crooked, looked straight at Billy the Brain. "I don't know how he did it, but Billy got that battery inside this fish so that I would win."

Judge Butterbar broke in. He took Craig by the shoulder and hugged him and that's when Craig whispered that he knew that God was watching him with one of his five billion eyes and Craig wanted everyone to know the truth. "Billy cheated for me. And the other guys helped me too."

"Billy! Did you cheat?" roars Judge Butterbar.

Billy the Brain looked back at the judges. His hair was still wet. "Of course I did," he says, proud as can be. "You bet I did."

The crowd roared. The Head of the Hall waved his arms and gave the 'silence' signal. "The Committee will take this entire matter under advisement," he says, very officially. "We will make a determination about the winner and announce our decision.....*tomorrow.*"

A huge moan shook the pier. Billy began to walk away, heading down the pier. We ran and grabbed him and pushed him against the rail. "Brain!" says Cal. "How'd you do it? How'd you get that battery in there?"

Billy said nothing. He was absolutely expressionless. "Come on, Billy! Tell us! How'd you get that big battery in that little fish?"

"Craig caught it that way. Crap, guys. I can't help what the fish eat around here."

"Come on, Billy."

"I didn't do nothing."

"Billy. God's watching you."

Billy looked back at us. He was a smart guy. "Of course he is. Why do you think I did it in the first place? Ain't that why we all cheated today?"

*****

The judges announced the winner at Monday lunch in the cafeteria. It was official. Craig Fairchild, Grand Champion, 1970. Craig the Cripple cried again. Happy tears this time. Craig was a hero. Billy's plan worked to perfection. Craig had the admiration of almost every last Hallboy. He beamed with pride and Craig would never have to wish he was like other kids again. His name is on the Grand Pacific Trophy. He finally owned one of the happiest memories a Hallboy could have, for the rest of his life. In the trophy case next to the trophy itself stands a photo of Craig the Cripple kneeling next to the goofiest halibut ever seen, with a car battery stuck inside.

*****

Billy never told a soul how he fit that huge battery inside the halibut. It's still a mystery. However, in doing so Billy the Brain revalidated his nickname and he changed the flavor of the Boys Hall Fishing Derby forever.

Cheating is still strictly forbidden at Boys Hall. After all, God has an eye on each and every one of us. So there is no cheating. <u>Except during</u>

the Derby. Starting the very next year, in honor of the *humanity* displayed by Billy the Brain and others, and for the strength showed by Craig Fairchild underneath God's ever-watching eyes, any amount of cheating during the Derby is now allowed. Cheating is not only acceptable during the Derby, it is *encouraged*. It's the only time of year when Hallboys may cheat.

This modification to the rules reminded us forever of Billy's incredible foresight. It also gave Hallboys a new outlet to express our creativity. We never ever learned how Billy the Brain got a car battery inside a halibut. The next year, I didn't even bring a fishing pole to the Derby. I carried a handful of water-proof cherry bombs and a five pound baby barbell to the end of the pier; I lit them all and dropped them in. They exploded under water, precisely as planned. I killed a whole bunch of fish, which all floated to the surface. But the biggest one was a six ounce sardine. Billy won the 1971 Derby with a Carp he stole from the Marineland Aquarium and stuffed it full of cobblestones from the beach.

*****

May, 2013
Scottsdale, Arizona

JOHNNY the ATOM TAKES OFF

Boys Hall

No Palms, California

April, 1972

Nobody liked pork chop night at Boys Hall in No Palms. Except for Billy the Brain. Billy scanned our trays in the big dining room for easy pickings. "I'm taking any and all uneaten pork chops," he said. "Pile 'em on."

I speared mine with my fork and deposited it on Billy's plate. "It's dry as dirt again. You can have it."

"Mine too," says Johnny the Atom as he handed his over as well, as did our pal Cal.

Billy stared happily at his little tower of chops, now stacked four high next to his mashed potatoes. That's when the Head of the Hall came into the room and held up his hand: the signal for silence. That meant, put down your fork and shut your mouth. There was going to be an announcement.

The Head of the Hall looked skinny under his baggy shirt and grey slacks. Never the most energetic man, nonetheless he cleared his throat like grinding rocks and says, for all to hear: "John McMartin. Please stand."

Our pal Johnny the Atom flinched. He glanced around at each of us, wiped mashed potatoes off his mouth, and pushed away from the table. Johnny the Atom was the fastest kid we knew, but he was in no hurry to stand up. Almost painfully, he pressed up and rose to his feet. The Head of the Hall nodded solemnly and said, "John, clear your tray and please come with me. Now."

We looked at each other and back to Johnny. An extraction in the middle of dinner was almost unheard of. Such an order from the Head of the Hall usually meant only one thing. Johnny was in big trouble. He got caught breaking the rules. The Head of the Hall stood in the doorway looking very serious as Johnny received the stares of over 200 Hallboys. We racked our brains, we exchanged whispers. What the heck had Johnny done? Johnny shrugged and laid his tray in the wash window and followed the Head of the Hall out the door.

We finished dinner and repaired to our rooms. We did our lessons. Johnny didn't return. After homework we gathered downstairs in the grand Parlor. Still no Johnny. Super weird, we thought. We'd played about 15 hands of poker when Johnny walked in. Hands in pockets. Dragging feet. Head hanging.

"Atom! Dude! What happened?"

"You guys ain't gonna believe it in a million years."

"What!?"

"Montana...." Johnny began to cry.

"Huh? Montana?"

"Yup," tears falling.

"Johnny....what is it?"

The Atom snuffled. "A family in Montana. They wanna adopt me."

*****

As Hallboys at Boys Hall in No Palms on the So Cal coast, we all understood that adoption was always a possibility. But almost never for us older kids. It was always the younger kids who were yanked away. The five and six year-olds. So for a 7th grader like Johnny to hear such news? That was wild.

Whenever a Hallboy got word of an adoption, mixed feelings ran amok. Typically the pending adoptee felt a surge of exhilaration. An enormous thrill came with the opportunity to go live with a real family, in a real house, to eat homemade food, to go to a real school, to have a real mom and dad. The good part was, of course, you were getting out of Boys Hall and No Palms. But the sad part, the crusher, especially in cases like Johnny the Atom, was the fact that you were leaving all your Hallboy pals. Your best friends. Your brothers.

Some kids felt a strange humility. After all, there was a certain amount of *flattery* involved. Somebody had chosen you. <u>You</u>. We knew there were albums in the office that contained all our pictures and backgrounds and profiles. But to pick you out, over hundreds of other Hallboys? Not to mention all the other "facilities" around. We knew there were hundreds or even thousands of other orphanages all around the country. How the heck had a set of parents narrowed their choice down to Boys Hall, for God's sake? And then, how'd they filter things all the way down to *you*?

And then, all the rest of us got sad. Whenever an adoption was announced, all us other Hallboys thought….each and every time…. Why Johnny? Why not <u>me</u>? Why didn't they pick *me*?"

*****

"What are you gonna do?" we asked Johnny.

The Hall's policy was clear, and I think it might have been a California law. After you reached the age of 12, the decision to go or to stay was strictly up to the kid.

"I think I'm gonna do it," the Atom told us. "I'm gonna go."

There was silence all around. Cal was first to speak. "Congratulations, Atom." Cal shook Johnny's hand. All adult-like.

"Dude. How cool for you," says Billy the Brain.

"You're a lucky guy," I told him. But inside, I honestly felt very little happiness. I was too caught up in my own sense of loss. I knew it was selfish but the feeling was there. My good pal was being taken away.

Johnny told us what he'd learned from the Head of the Hall. A family in Montana. They lived on a ranch. Small town, like No Palms. While No Palms had its beach and ocean, Montana had mountains and streams. There was a regular school with sports teams. We all knew that Johnny would fit right in with the sports, because he was so fast. There were chores at the ranch. We knew that wouldn't bother Johnny a bit.

*****

The next Saturday morning Johnny's new mom and dad came to Boys Hall to meet him and take Johnny away. We were out front, mowing the big lawn with the dreaded push-mowers, when a big car pulled up to the front of the Hall.

"Look," says Billy. "It's a rental. They do it all the time. The big old rental car trick. They always show up with the biggest car they can find."

The Head of the Hall came out but stood back, staying up on the steps. Johnny's new dad got out of the car. He wore jeans and cowboy boots. He put on a cowboy hat, stood back with his hands on hips, facing the Hall. I had to admit. He looked like a cool dad. Then the mom got out. She wore boots too. Big smile. Happy.

Johnny stepped forward. He walked right up to the dad. I was so proud of him. He put out his hand and said, very smartly, "Hi. I'm John McMartin."

The dad took off his cowboy hat. They shook hands. He didn't try to be a big shot or anything. He just spoke a few words and he introduced the mom. They shook hands too.

Then nobody said much of anything. So Johnny the Atom looked up at them and says, "Did you want to meet my friends?"

"Yes! Of course."

And Johnny introduced me and Cal and Billy. We shook hands all round and saw their gracious smiles. Then the Head of the Hall walked over and said Hello and took Johnny and his new mom and dad into the main building, into the Head of the Hall's office. They stayed in there for over 90 minutes, getting acquainted, while we wrestled those awful push-mowers back and forth across the great lawn.

*****

When a Hallboy is adopted, an awkward tradition at Boys Hall is the final ceremonial lunch in the dining room. This is just another cruddy lunch to most of the boys, unless you happen to be a good friend of the adoptee. The new mom and dad sit at the same table with their new son, along with all his best friends. So there we were. Johnny, me, Cal, Billy, Craig, a few others, the mom and dad, and the Head of the Hall. All sitting around a table in the center of the big room.

"You like to ride horses," the dad started out.

"I never did that," says Johnny.

"Wanna try?"

"Sure."

The mom took a stack of pictures out of her purse and passed them around. Whoa. Story-book. They lived on a ranch alright. Horses, a corral, a big handsome log house. It was kind of pretty. A pond. Cows. Dogs too!

"We have two other children," the mom said to Johnny. Brian and Julie." She handed Johnny the Atom a photo. "Here's our son. He's exactly your age. Twelve. And here's our daughter. She's fourteen." We looked at the photographs. Johnny's new sister had a cowboy hat too. The kids sat on a wooden fence with trees and mountain peaks in the distance. It looked as if it were a million miles from No Palms.

I felt a crappy trickle of envy go through my body. Cal said it best. "Take me too!" I felt my guts jump. Whoa! Was I about to lose both Johnny and Cal?

The lunch conversation around the table started off well enough, but after the pictures were handed around the talking slowed way down. We ate our ham sandwiches in mostly silence. Johnny finished first. His last lunch. The mom and dad exchanged glances a couple times and the dad tried to keep the conversation peppy. He talked about the school, and something about winter and skiing. "And there's fishing in a few streams near our home."

"That's something we're all pretty good at," I put in. "Here in No Palms, we fish off the old pier all the time."

The dad smiled at me and finished his sandwich. That's when he said, "And John. In our house, you'll have your very own room, all to yourself! How's that sound?"

I looked at Cal. This was a downright stupid thing to say at a Hall-boy lunch, where every one of us had a roommate and where we'd shared a room with another Hallboy since our very first day. And the dad knew it was a stupid thing to say. He suddenly looked sheepish. This gave us a reason to hate him. Besides the fact that he was taking our pal away.

"Boys," says the dad. "You'll have to come up and visit. Ride horses. We'll have us some camping and a big chuck-wagon cook-out. I'll make all the arrangements."

Yeah, sure. We'd all heard this sort of thing before. Many times. And we all knew one thing: it would never happen. Every adopting family promised this stuff. Did it ever happen? Not once. Nada.

I felt sad. In the end, everyone wanted lunch to be over and to get on with it. Get it over with. Be done.

*****

Johnny the Atom was packed. Everything he owned went into three bags. I gave him my old Indian pocket knife. It was really cool but I told him, "Take this, Johnny. You can use it there on the ranch. There in the mountains."

The Head of the Hall said it was time to get in the car and go to the airport. We slowly assembled back in front of the main building and when Johnny's three bags went into the trunk I felt my stomach buckle.

The dad opened the car door.

"Bye, Atom."

"Good for you."

"Hallboys forever."

And we joined in a five-way hug.

"Yep." We all sniffled. "Hallboys forever."

Cal, Billy, Craig and I stood stone still as Johnny got into the big car. I felt dazed. The mom smiled. The dad waved. The car doors closed. Johnny the Atom waved weakly as the car slowly pulled away, rounding the drive, heading for the gates, with me and Cal and Billy and Craig running behind, tears on our cheeks.

I remember dinner that night. It stunk.

*****

After Johnny left, life at Boys Hall stumbled on. The day after he left I remember how we went to the library and pulled out the World Book and an atlas to look up Montana. We learned so much. Montana, of course, was full of high mountains and America's widest prairies. Part of Yellowstone was in Montana. Bears lived there. And buffalo. Its history was one of pioneer exploration, Lewis and Clark, and dangerous Indians. General Custer got smeared there. Montana had 15 or 20 kinds of trout. It was vastly more colorful than dull little old No Palms with our creaking pier and a park and old people and the lame shops. Montana had glaciers and roaring rivers and cowboys and moose and huge ranches.

"People ride horses in Montana instead of cars," says Cal.

"It snows there in the winter," Billy the Brain adds. "I betcha they have blizzards and even avalanches."

Cal clipped a small Montana flag out of the encyclopedia and pasted it on his wall, over his desk, to remind him of Johnny the Atom and Montana. I got an old western bandana from one of the goodwill stores downtown. For a week or so, it was my link, my connection with Johnny. But as time passed, and as life went on, the memory of Johnny the Atom slid behind us. Spring warmed into summer and we started thinking about our beach again. We got ready for tests and baseball games and for the Fishing Derby. The truth was that we talked about Johnny the Atom less and less, until, I gotta admit, several days would go by when we'd never even think about him.

One day in late June the Head of the Hall handed me an envelope. It was addressed to me and Cal and Billy and Craig. Return address: Montana. A letter from the Atom.

Dear Chip and Cal and Billy and Craig,

Hello from Montana. I live near some big peaks which are part of the Rocky Mountains. Our house is sort of in the wilderness, but sort of near a little town which is about as big as No Palms. But it's much different than the beach. The Jones live on a ranch like you saw in the pictures. We raise cattle. They eat the hay and grass that grows wild on the range. The Jones don't eat the hay. The cattle do.

We have a big fireplace in our house, just like at Boys Hall. My new brother is nice. So is my sister. She has nice friends who come over a lot. It's weird to be around girls so much, but like I said, they are all nice. My sister cooks with my mom. They bake a plate of cookies almost every day. I shoulda sent you some.

I have a horse here for my very own. Its name is Taco. My brother and sister have taught me to ride and stuff. We ride after school almost every day. I can saddle up a horse like I been doing it for years. I can gallop and ride a horse through a river. You should see my boots. And my cowboy hat!!!

We have three dogs. A skunk wandered into the yard two days ago. The dogs went batshit. One of them got blasted. That was fun.

School is okay. I think I'm the fastest kid in the class. Are the stupid old bats at the Women Club still wrecking No Palms? Oh well. Guess I'd better go now.

John.

Me and Cal and Billy and Craig finished the letter and looked at each other.

All our weird feelings flooded back to us.

"Lucky bastard."

"Jackpot for Johnny."

"His very own horse?"

"And a cowboy hat?" I said, looking at my faded and frayed purple Hallboy cap. "Dang."

"Oh well," Cal looked at me. "Good for Johnny."

"Yeah. Good for Johnny."

But I'm not sure any of us really meant it.

*****

Three Saturdays later we were doing front lawn chores. The No Palms fog was pretty thick. It was Billy's turn to do the push-mower while Cal and I scraped splotches of sea-gull poop off the driveway. A taxi-cab pulled through the gates and stopped in front of the purple main doors of Boys Hall. Johnny the Atom got out and dropped a small duffle bag on the driveway.

"Johnny!"

"Atom-man!"

"You're back!"

"Yeah."

"For a visit?"

The cab driver came round the car and set down two more bags.

"Nope. I'm back for good."

"Huh? **Dude**!"

"Yep."

"What happened? You didn't like it?"

"No. I mean, I did. I really liked it. It's a cool place. There was no complaints."

"You liked Montana?"

"Oh. Dudes. Montana is great!"

"Your new dad?"

"He's really nice."

"The mom?"

"She's wonderful. So is my brother and sister. It's a very nice family."

"The food?"

"Terrific. Gawd! I never ate so good."

"The new school. I bet it was a drag being the new guy."

"Not really. School was okay."

"Then what happened?"

"The dogs. The horses. It was so cool."

"Johnny. But you're back. So what happened?"

"I'm…I'm not really sure. I just had these *feelings,* you know?"

"Feelings?"

"Yeah. One night I was sitting in the living room with my father. Mom brought us pie. We watched TV. And I just blurted it out. 'Dad. I'm sorry. But I think I want to go back to Boys Hall'."

"Whoa!" Cal clapped. "I'll bet that bent his brain! What did your dad say?"

"He asks me, 'Are you sure?' I said, 'Yeah, dad. I'm certain. I'm sure I'm sure. I want to go back'."

Billy the Brain leaned on the push mower and shook his head. "Johnny. You're crazy. They shoulda picked me."

"You woulda gone?" asked Cal.

"You bet! I'd love Montana."

"Really?"

"Yeah. For about two weeks. Ha!"

"Chip," Johnny says to me, "here's your knife back. I skinned a skunk with it. The knife still stinks."

"Perfect."

Johnny the Atom wasn't the first Hallboy to leave for a real family home, only to come back to Boys Hall. A few actually returned to the Hall and its crappy food, its dirty bathrooms with cold showers and toilets that didn't always flush; the fog, the cruddy basketballs and the push mowers and the seagull poop. Not to mention the long boring walk into No Palms and the creaky pier.

Every one of us *dreamed* for a real family out there to notice us, then to choose us, to ask to take us away. But very very few of us were truly ready to leave.

"I'll help you guys finish the chores," Johnny the Atom said. "After that, is El Burger Bucket still open? You guys want to go downtown and get a shake?"

"Yes!" I cheered.

"Atom," Cal asked. "Why'd you come back?"

"I told you. I really don't know."

"Huh?"

"I really don't know. But up there, as nice as everything was, it just wasn't the same."

We shook hands and hugged Johnny back home. I felt terrific. Our pal was back.

"Hey," says Johnny the Atom, out there on the front lawn, taking his turn with the mower. Then he stopped mowing and turned to us, with some questions.

"Dudes. I been gone almost five months. Did they ever fix the big TV in the Parlor?"

"What do you think? It's still broke."

"Does the Head of the Hall still snore when he's awake?"

"Louder than ever."

"And tell me this. Are we still at war with the Women's Club?"

"Hell Yeah!" says Billy. "I've got a whole flat of eggs rotting under my bed right now."

"Bitchen. It's so great to be home."

*****

Scottsdale Arizona

May, 2015

****

For more about Chip Rock and No Palms, the epic novel
CHIP ROCK and the FAT OLD FART, is as good as it gets.

For more information about all Mike's Books, please go to
www.michaeldaswick.com

Made in the USA
Columbia, SC
12 September 2019